Wal

I Think
I'll Just
Curl Up and
DIE!

I Think I'll Just Curl Up and Die!

ROSIE RUSHTON

Piccadilly Press • London

For Niki, Sally and Caroline – as inspiring as ever!

First published in Great Britain in 1995
by Piccadilly Press Ltd,
5 Castle Road, London NW1 8PR
www.piccadillypress.co.uk

This edition reissued 2006

A catalogue record for this book is available from the British Library

ISBN: 1 85340 892 1 (trade paperback)
EAN: 9 781853 408922

1 3 5 7 9 10 8 6 4 2

Chapter One

Home Thoughts From Abroad

Dear Jemma,

Guess what? I'm in love! He's seventeen, his name is Bilu and we met at my cousin's wedding. He is amazing! He's got these gorgeous eyes and he is really cool. The best bit of all is that even Dad thinks he's wonderful! So I'm allowed to see him. This afternoon we're all going to watch the polo and tonight he wants to take me to the cinema. (I know I said I don't like Indian films, but with him I'd watch them in Ancient Greek!)

No time to write more - I've got to decide what to wear. Tell Laura she's welcome to Jon - I prefer older boys. By the way, I'm growing my hair long again. Bilu likes long hair.

See you soon! Isn't love wonderful?

Sumitha xxx

Jemma Farrant sighed and tossed the postcard on to the bed. How would she know whether love was wonderful or not? She'd never had a boyfriend – not that she would dare bring one home to meet her mother if she did get lucky. Jemma had only recently persuaded her mother to let her choose her own clothes; if Mrs Farrant had her way she would still be wearing cord pinafores and smocked

1

dresses. As for boys, Jemma's mum insisted that fourteen was far too young to be consorting with males. If Jemma did meet a boy, her mother would probably invite him round for jelly and ice cream and a nice quiet game of Snakes and Ladders.

When Jemma had started at Lee Hill school, she had seen Sumitha as something of a kindred spirit. While Jemma had problems with an overprotective mother with all the fashion sense of a Stone Age hermit, Sumitha was always at odds with her dad. He was really strict and nearly went mental when Sumitha had her hair cut without permission. He even thought that The Stomping Ground, where anyone who wanted to get a life in Leehampton went on a Saturday night, was a den of iniquity to be avoided at all costs. And yet it seemed he had accepted this new boyfriend of Sumitha's with open arms.

She picked up the postcard and re-read it. It can't last, she comforted herself. After all, he's in India and Sumitha lives here. Jemma thought of her other friends. Chelsea had her sights firmly set on Rob Antell, Laura lusted after Jon and now Sumitha was in love. She didn't fancy being the only one left with no one to swoon over.

Jemma was also bored. Her dad had said they couldn't have a family holiday this year because of just having moved house and him starting a new job. He told her that the school trip to Paris would have to do and she should count her blessings. It had been brilliant – seven whole days without her mother clucking around – but it was over

2

now. What's more, he had just forked out a vast sum of money to join the new Waterline Golf and Leisure Club. This was good in some ways because they had a huge pool and Jacuzzis and a water chute, which the family could use while Mr Farrant was out trying to be the next Tiger Woods. However it had its grim side because Jemma's mum disported herself in the water wearing a ghastly swimsuit with a frilly skirt and shrieking 'Take care, petals,' at Jemma and her siblings at ten second intervals to the amusement of everyone but Jemma.

She looked at herself critically in her bedroom mirror. She hated her sludge coloured hair and loathed her front teeth which stuck out a bit. She was feeling fat and lumpy. All those croissants and wedges of Camembert cheese had taken their toll, most of it between her boobs and her belly button. And talking of boobs, over the past few months hers appeared to have taken on a life of their own, expanding at an alarming rate. She'd have to get a better bra; her dear mother still bought those awful beginner things that looked like two eggshells on a piece of elastic and had about as much effect.

'Why can't I look like Chelsea?' she thought, yanking her hair into a pink elastic. 'I bet she's being chatted up by every Spaniard within a ten mile radius. And what's more, her mum won't care at all. Life just isn't fair.'

Chapter Two

Wanna Be Loved

This sentiment, it seemed, was shared by Chelsea herself, or so it would seem from the letter which her friend, Laura Turnbull received on Tuesday.

Chez Calypso, Estepona, Spain

Dear Laura,

I'm sitting on our balcony praying that my mother doesn't find me. You won't believe the day I have just had! I have never been so embarrassed in my entire life.

This morning, while I was playing volleyball with these cool guys I met at the hotel club, a woman came swanning along the beach with a guy holding a camera and another with one of those furry microphone things they use for street interviews. They were filming for one of those holiday programmes on the television - and who did they home in on? My mother! Of course, you can guess she loved it - all that attention. She acted like Liz Hurley. They filmed her learning to get up on the surfboard, falling off, shrieking with delight - the works. It was awful. Then they said they wanted a shot of her actually surfing over the waves - and she couldn't

4

do it! She kept falling off. They gave up in the end. You would think that would have been enough to shut her up but no. 'Come and meet my daughter,' she says. I could have killed her. This gorgeous guy Juan was just beginning to come on strong when up comes my mother and drags me off to be filmed at the barbecue. We had to stand there for ages, munching on sardines and saying why we thought Chez Calypso was the idyllic holiday venue.

And the hypocrisy of my mother! 'Oh, there's such a lot to keep Chelsea amused!' she simpers, right into the camera. 'What with the Teenscene Club' (I've never been to the stupid thing) 'and the Killer Darts' (I only play when she threatens me with no club if I don't keep Dad happy) 'and lots of lovely young people.' (And then when I say I am going off to the market on Juan's motorbike, she comes the heavy-handed mother and talks about drugs and date rape.)

Juan is amazing - he has this gorgeous tan and jet black hair and he says he thinks I am the most beautiful girl he has ever seen. That guy's got taste!

If they show that film on TV I shall die. It's enough having Mum spouting away on local radio every week - but national television! It doesn't bear thinking about. I wonder if I could refuse consent on the grounds of infringement of privacy ... it's worth a try.

5

Hope you had a great time in France and got the
Bestial Betsy sorted once and for all. See you when
I get back - you can tell all then.

Loads of love
Chelsea

Laura sat in the middle of a pile of dirty washing, reading
Chelsea's letter and giggling. She could just imagine how
irate Chelsea would be at her mother's antics, although
why she got so fazed by it, she couldn't imagine. Laura
thought that Mrs Gee was a real laugh — not a bit mother-
like. It would be a blast seeing her on the television. She
was always doing mad things, and she never seemed to
worry about whether Chelsea was getting enough vita-
mins or whether women her size should really wear bright
orange shorts. I suppose that's what comes of being an
agony aunt and journalist, thought Laura. You stop caring
what everyone else thinks and just do your own thing.

Come to think of it, though, most parents did that, one
way or another. Hers certainly had. Her mother obviously
didn't care one bit about her reputation when she carried
on in public with toyboy Melvyn, and her father showed
no regret for having moved in with the Bestial Betsy and
her sad kids.

Laura sighed. She had thought that, given time, her
mum would see sense and ask her dad to move back in.
She had assumed that Dad was just waiting for the chance.

But it hadn't happened. Her mum was still wrapped up in the geek Melvyn and she hadn't even seemed to mind Laura going off camping in France with Dad and the Bestial Betsy. And those two were all over each other; it made you want to throw up.

She kicked a flip flop under the bed. Life was very unjust. Never mind her ageing parents – she was the one who needed a love life. She'd got to the bit in The Novel (the one she'd been writing for months and which was going to make her a household name) where the hero seduces the heroine behind the greenhouse in the manor garden. The problem was, never having been seduced, Laura was afraid some of the detail might be wrong. What she needed was first hand research. She fancied Jon Joseph like crazy but, to date, he hadn't exactly fallen over himself to be with her. Of course, it could be that Sumitha was right and that he was so overcome with passion that he couldn't bring himself to confront his own emotions. Perhaps if she went over to Jemma's house, she might bump into him – he did live next door to Jemma, after all.

Consoling herself with thoughts of a joyous reunion, she kicked the washing into the corner and started varnishing her toenails.

Chapter Three

The Art of Love

By Wednesday, the object of Laura's affections was battling with the design of a strip cartoon, the final assignment of the masterclass with Blob at the Dellfield Activity Holiday Centre. It had been a fantastic week and Jon was now more sure than ever that he wanted to be a political cartoonist.

The course leader – who was really called Eric Batterby, but who used Blob as his pen name – leaned over the table where Jon was working and handed him a pile of sketches which had been his last assignment.

'Good work, Jon. Liked it a lot. Who's the funky girl with the bike in this one? Oh, and by the way, that cartoon of the Prime Minister and the fishing fleet was very funny.'

Jon looked at the top sketch in surprise. He knew he doodled all the time, but he had no recollection of doing this one. It was that kid – the one who'd knocked him off his bike back in the summer term. The one who'd kept staring at him that night at the club. Laura someone. Mind you, her face had always interested him. It had a kind of 'mess with me at your peril' look and yet her eyes were soft and vulnerable. He'd love to sketch her portrait.

Get real, he told himself firmly. What was he thinking about? The only girl he was even mildly interested in was Sumitha. Next term, he would find a way of asking her out.

'I'll see you later, Jon' said the tutor. 'I'm meeting your father for a beer at lunchtime.'

Jon's heart sank. Doubtless Dad would do his 'Now I hope you realise my son is something special,' routine and make a complete fool of himself. Even though he had come round to the idea that Jon was not going to go to Cambridge or become a lawyer, he couldn't seem to stop bragging to the world about his son's prowess. On the first day, he had cornered Eric and told him that he was lucky to have such a talented lad in his class. Jon had nearly died. Why couldn't he stick to his Golf Improvers course and forget about his son for once?

Still, the tutor liked his stuff. He was on his way to being a proper artist. And when he got back, he'd ask Sumitha out. Fired with confidence, Jon began drawing himself as Orlando Bloom, surrounded by swooning girls.

Chapter Four

All Good Things Come to an End

In the early hours of Thursday morning, Rajiv Banerji was tapping his foot impatiently as the baggage carousel in the arrivals hall at Heathrow airport jerked into life.

'I hope we don't have to wait too long,' he said, looking

at his watch, 'I want to get home to open my post and sort out my rotas and plan next Tuesday's meeting.'

'Calm down, Rajiv,' said his wife, laying a hand on his arm. 'You've had a lovely holiday – no need to get all worked up and stressed out again so soon.'

He smiled. 'Yes, all in all, it was a good break,' he admitted, grabbing hold of little Sandeep who was about to leap on to the carousel. 'And so good that Sumitha has seen how life is in India.' He glanced over to where his daughter was perched on her rucksack listening to her iPod with a dreamy expression on her face.

'That nice boy Bilu is just what she needs – and from such a good family too. He'll knock all this Western nonsense out of her head. She's already saying she is going to grow her hair long again,' he added, looking at his wife in smug satisfaction. Somehow he felt that she had not backed him enough on the issue of Sumitha and the haircut.

Chitrita Banerji inclined her head, smiled but said nothing. She had watched from the window as Sumitha and Bilu had said goodbye to one another at her mother's house the previous day, and as a result, right now, it was not her daughter's hair she was worried about.

Sumitha, meanwhile, was staring dreamily into space, reliving her first kiss from Bilu under the margosa tree in her grandmother's garden.

Chapter Five
Money Is the Root of All Rows

Late on Friday evening, in Thorburn Crescent, Ginny Gee was wondering how two weeks living in a swimsuit and a couple of sarongs could produce so much laundry, when the bell rang.

'I'll get it,' yelled Chelsea who had seen Rob cycling into the Crescent.

'Hi!' she said, grinning broadly, and hoping that her suntan made her look entirely irresistible.

'Hiya,' said Rob. 'Is your Mum in?'

'Yes,' sighed Chelsea, running her fingers through her chestnut curls, 'but she's busy.' It's me you're supposed to be after, not her, she thought irritably. This wasn't how the boys in Spain reacted to her – there it was all wolf whistles and bottom pinching and here she was being practically ignored by the boy of her dreams.

'Well, hello there Rob, and how are you?' gushed Ginny, coming downstairs with an armful of washing.

'Did you have a good holiday, Mrs Gee?' asked Rob.

'Now, how many times have I told you? It's Ginny,' said Chelsea's mum, smiling.

'Ginny,' said Rob. 'I just wondered if you could have a look at my entry for the Leehampton Young Writers' Competition – I'm not too sure about the ending.'

'Sure, no problem,' said Ginny. 'Leave it on the table and I'll give it a look over the weekend.'

'GINNY!' Barry Gee yelled from the confines of the kitchen. 'What in the name of heaven is this?'

Chelsea's mum cringed.

'Oh dear, probs.' She smiled. 'Chelsea, why don't you take Rob upstairs and I'll bring you up drinks in a moment?'

About time too, thought Chelsea, showing Rob the way.

Ginny took a deep breath and walked into the kitchen.

Her husband was standing there surrounded by three headless trout and a pile of what looked like sliced canvas. They hadn't even finished unpacking and he was back in Amateur Chef of the Year mode, thought Ginny wryly. What was more worrying was the rather vicious way in which he was waving a Barclaycard bill in the air.

'I found this,' he said shortly.

'Ah yes,' said Ginny. 'Well, it came the day we left for Spain and I didn't want to spoil the holiday atmosphere so I . . .'

'So you hid it in the toaster – brilliant!' said Barry. 'Ginny, this bill is for £1,396. What in the name of goodness has been going on?'

'Well, these things mount up,' began Ginny, wishing she had had the foresight to put the bill in her knicker drawer. 'You know how it is.'

'Frankly, no. Half this stuff is totally unnecessary,'

snapped Barry, scanning his eyes over the list of purchases. 'You are simply going to have to cut back.'

'Well, if you got a job, maybe I wouldn't have to,' shouted Ginny. 'If you spent more time job hunting and less time messing about with gourmet recipes, we might be better off.'

Barry had been feeling rather guilty about his lack of success in the job hunting stakes and didn't need reminding of the fact by his wife.

'I have an image to keep up – I'm in the public eye,' continued Ginny. This last year she had discovered that it takes a lot of hard work to look good when bits of you that you forgot you had started flopping and sagging all over the place. Getting older was not something Ginny could easily accommodate.

'Oh yes, I forgot – the local rag demands that its feature writer dresses solely in Joseph and Karen Millen, does it? And of course, when you're on the radio, everyone can see your designer gear, can't they? Well, we have a house to run and Warwick to put through university and . . .'

Upstairs, Chelsea heard the rising tones of unrest and firmly shut her bedroom door.

'Did you miss me?' she asked Rob.

'What? Oh – er, yes, course I did' said Rob. 'What with Jon away too, there was no one to have a laugh with.'

Laughing was not precisely what Chelsea had in mind.

Still, nothing ventured, nothing gained. What was it her mother was always going on about? 'If you want something in this life, Chelsea, you have to go out and make darned sure you get it.'

She leaned over and kissed Rob on the lips. He looked surprised – although not totally displeased. But he didn't kiss her back.

'Rob, you do like me, don't you?' said Chelsea.

'What? Oh, er, yes – of course I do,' replied Rob, suddenly showing an intense interest in his thumbnails. 'You're cool.'

Chelsea felt a warm glow. As romantic avowals went it might not win prizes but it was the best she'd received to date.

Maybe things were looking up, she thought.

In the kitchen things were definitely on the downward slope.

'OK, OK, no need to go on,' Ginny snapped. 'Anyway, while you're so busy criticising everything I do, what about you? When are you going to cut back on all this designer food?' She waved a tanned hand in the general direction of the trout. Barry glanced at them in surprise, as if they had just surfaced from a nearby stream and placed themselves in his kitchen.

'Ah – but if I am going to enter the ITV *Superchef* competition, I need to work with quality ingredients,' said Barry hurriedly. 'A couple of pheasants and the odd pound of okra once in a while is hardly the same as a clutch of designer suits and the odd Prada handbag!'

Ginny sighed. 'OK, OK, I'll make a pact with you. I'll cut back on my personal spending if you make a real effort to find work. Any work. Soon. Like tomorrow. OK?'

'OK,' sighed Barry. He had really quite enjoyed his ten months at home since Freshfoods made him redundant. He'd never been one of these high flying chaps with their eye on the boardroom. Give him a pile of pasta and a few prawns and he was happy to create culinary delights all morning. If only people would pay him for inventing twenty things to do with a haddock. But Ginny was right. He'd have to do something.

They would all have to do something or they would be in the soup. Hang on a minute. Now that was a good idea . . .

Chapter Six

Love Is in the Air

'So come on, Sumitha, tell us *everything*!' said Chelsea. It was the last Saturday of the holidays and the first chance she had had to get together with her friends and catch up on all the gossip. The venue was Jemma's bedroom, because Laura was hoping for a glimpse of Jon. This explained why she was sitting on the windowsill getting pins and needles in her bottom and a crick in her neck from swivelling her head every ten seconds to peer into his front garden.

'What about this amazing guy?' encouraged Laura. 'Jemma said you liked him even better than Jon – do you really?' she added hopefully.

Sumitha flopped down on Jemma's floor cushions, ran her fingers through her hair, and sighed.

'He is,' she said, 'just divine. He's seventeen, has a body to die for, a wonderful smile and,' she paused for maximum effect, 'a car.'

'Wow!' said Chelsea, 'Is he rich?'

'Uh-huh.' Sumitha nodded. 'And next weekend,' she added dreamily, 'he's staying at our house.'

'How come?' asked Laura, frowning. 'I thought he lived in Calcutta.'

'No, his family just spend the summer holidays there with the grandparents. His mum and dad live in London but they travel a lot, and guess what?'

Everyone looked expectant.

'Bilu is a boarder in the Sixth Form at – you won't believe this – Bellborough Court!'

That it *so* not on, thought Jemma. She'll get to see him all the time, I'll be the only one left without a boy.

'That's where Jon goes,' interrupted Laura, her interest suddenly increasing ten fold.

Sumitha glared at her. For once she had centre stage and she was not about to give it up to Laura.

'Yes, well, my dad was talking to Bilu's dad at my cousin's wedding and it came up in conversation. So Dad said he could stay with us some weekends when his parents were away.'

'But I thought your parents were really iffy about boyfriends,' said Jemma, clutching at straws.

'That's the great thing,' said Sumitha, hugging her knees in excitement. 'Because his family are related by marriage to my cousin's aunt, or something like that, Dad sees him as part of our extended family. And he keeps saying that it is good for me to have the company of a "nicely brought up Bengali boy who shares our standards".' She giggled. 'He might not say that if he had seen us at the *mela*.'

'The what?' said Chelsea, abstractedly picking pink nail polish off her big toe.

'Oh, it's a fair they have for Rathajatra – to celebrate the monsoon rains coming,' said Sumitha. 'Everyone goes and Bilu took me – well, the whole family went actually, but we gave them the slip.' She giggled. 'Bilu bought me jasmine flowers and held my hand.'

'So you really like him?' said Laura, wishing that Jon had held her hand just once.

'I am,' said Sumitha, 'deeply, passionately in love.'

Great, thought Laura. That's Sumitha out of the way. From now on, I can have Jon all to myself. All she had to do now was convince Jon of that fact.

'So when are we going to get to meet this guy?' asked

Jemma. Perhaps he'd be really gormless and ugly and then she wouldn't feel so bad.

'Why don't we all go to The Stomping Ground on Saturday and Sumitha can bring him!' said Laura, giggling. And I might get to see Jon, she added silently.

'Great idea,' agreed Chelsea.

Sumitha was not at all sure she wanted to share one second of Bilu's stay with anyone else – but on the other hand, it would be ace to be able to show him off. Her very own boyfriend – and one with a car at that.

'How was Brittany, Laura?' asked Jemma, suddenly eager to get away from the subject of boyfriends. 'Did you manage to dispose of the Bestial Betsy?'

'No chance,' said Laura gloomily. 'That woman is seriously weird. She kept dashing off to markets to buy oysters and weird cheeses that smelled like cow's dung, and she wears flowers in her hair and has conversations with trees. Insane or what?'

'What are her kids like?' asked Jemma.

'Beyond wet,' declared Laura. 'Mind you, with a mother like that, what chance have they got? There was this huge row one night because Sonia wouldn't let Daryl – who's so uncool you wouldn't believe – play ping pong. My dad told her to grow up and she went mental. I mean, seriously. She yelled at him and said, "You're not my dad, and you can't tell me what to do!" and when my dad tried to reason with her, she just screeched that she hated the lot of us and wished she was dead. Then she ran off.'

'So what happened?' asked Sumitha.

'I went to look for her – to get away from Betsy's wittering on about the poor little soul and what a rotten so-and-so my dad was to annoy her. I found her on the beach howling her eyes out. I couldn't help feeling a bit sorry for her – after all, she's only eleven. She was sitting there, hurling bits of shell in to the sea and saying how much she hated my dad, and how she wished he would disappear forever and how her mum ought to know better than to take up with a man like him.'

'Sounds pretty much like what you say about your mum and Melvyn,' commented Chelsea.

'Well, I know, but I mean – you simply can't compare my dad with that geek, can you?' demanded Laura. 'My dad's way intelligent, and brilliant fun and she's blimmin' lucky to have him.'

'Well, at least your dad is happy,' said Jemma soothingly.

'Yes, but now my mother's acting all weird. I only have to say half a word and she snaps my head off. She moons around all morning in a dressing gown looking pallid. Actually, what I'm hoping is that she's had a big bust up with the idiot Melvyn while I was away. She hasn't said anything, but she's been really quiet.'

'That's a bit rough on your mum,' said Chelsea, who secretly couldn't see what was wrong with Melvyn.

'No, it's not!' shouted Laura. 'It's time she saw sense. She'll get over it, and anyway, he was never right for her.'

'Says who?' asked Jemma, a tad ill-advisedly.

'Says me!' snapped Laura. 'It's all right for you. Your mum and dad are together. You,' she added emphatically, 'are not the traumatised child of a broken home.'

The others said nothing. They all knew better than to tackle Laura when she was having a drama-queen moment.

'Did you meet any dishy guys in Paris, Jemma?' asked Sumitha, for whom any conversation that didn't offer the chance to extol Bilu's virtues held little interest.

'Not really,' admitted Jemma reluctantly. 'Not that I didn't chat to loads of cool guys,' she added hastily, 'but it's a bit difficult to get off with someone when Mr Horage hovers over you like a sentry and Miss McConnell keeps marching you off to see more museums.'

'Bor-ing!' said Sumitha, doing a mock yawn behind her hands.

'No, it was good fun really,' insisted Jemma. 'It was just so great not having Mum clucking over me like a headless chicken all the time. Mind you, she's making up for lost time now. I've found this cool diet to go on and now my mum thinks I'm going to fade away to nothing.' She paused, hoping that everyone would chorus 'Oh but Jemma, you've got a lovely figure, you don't need to diet!' They didn't.

'What about this guy that you met in Spain?' Sumitha asked Chelsea, deftly steering the conversation back to boys, 'Does that mean you've gone off Rob?'

'No way,' said Chelsea. 'Rob's much nicer. Juan was just useful for the holidays. He followed me everywhere – it was quite cute. And he kept buying me drinks and chocolate – he even bought me flowers one time.'

'Wow!' said Jemma. Why couldn't someone buy her flowers?

'Anyway,' said Chelsea, tossing her chestnut curls and pursing her lips, 'I got fed up with him – he was only after one thing.'

The others looked impressed. To date, no one had been after anything with them other than a share of their French fries.

'You mean . . . ?' said Laura.

'So what happened?' enquired Sumitha, who felt it might be as well to find out more on these matters.

'Nothing,' said Chelsea airily, 'I told him to get lost.'

The others nodded in approval.

'You've got to be really in love for that,' said Laura, with the voice of one who knows.

'I'd be scared,' said Jemma, honest as ever.

'You will know when you have met the right person,' intoned Sumitha, wrapping her arms round her chest and giving herself a little hug. 'You just know.'

Chelsea said nothing. She wasn't going to let on that Juan had told her he was tired of going round with a kid. A girl has her pride. 'Should be good this term,' she said brightly in an attempt to divert the conversation away from the passion she wished she could've got a taste of. 'What with *Oliver!* and everything. Are you going to audition for the Artful Dodger like Mr Horage suggested, Sumitha?'

21

'I might,' said Sumitha. 'But only if they don't have any rehearsals at weekends, because Bilu will want me to be free to see him.'

At that moment, Mrs Farrant appeared at the bedroom door. 'Thought you might be peckish, petals,' she cooed. 'I've bought you up some snacks and some drinks.'

'Thanks, Mrs Farrant,' they chorused.

'Oh MUM!' said Jemma, as her mother placed the tray on the bedside table. 'Not animal biscuits! Puh-lease!'

Chapter Seven
I Don't Like Mondays

Monday morning brought about a mixture of high hopes and rude awakenings in several households in Leehampton. At 47 Billing Hill, Jon Joseph was gulping his breakfast in the hope of being out of the house before his father launched into his usual first-day-of-term pep talk about consolidated effort, aiming high and buckling down. Dad may have finally accepted that his son had no wish to go to Cambridge and wanted to do art instead, but that didn't stop him exhorting him to hit the heights and put Lowry in the shade.

His father, however, appeared to have other things on his mind.

'I can't find my red pinstripe shirt!' Henry Joseph bellowed down the stairwell.

'It's in the ironing basket,' replied his wife Anona calmly, wondering why it was that her husband needed to exercise his vocal chords as if trying to communicate with Belgium.

'But I need it today!' Henry bumbled into the kitchen, looking faintly ridiculous in a pair of green boxer shorts and yellow socks.

'So iron it,' replied his wife mildly, ticking off a list as she packed her bag.

Henry stopped dead in his tracks. 'But you always iron on Sundays,' he said.

'So this week I didn't,' said Mrs Joseph, turning to him. 'If you remember, I start my Interior Design course today and I have had more important things to think about than whether the household laundry is up to scratch. Now where did I put those new pastels?'

'Now look here, Anona,' blustered Henry, his fat cheeks taking on a somewhat mulberry hue. 'I've got a job to go to. Who is it who will be bringing home the cash now that you've decided to opt out of the job market?'

'You, dear, for the time being,' replied his wife calmly. 'Ah, there they are.'

'Precisely!' expostulated Henry smugly. 'And just because you're doing some course, you can't expect me to go to work in an unironed shirt.'

'Of course not, Henry my sweet. As if I would,' Mrs

Joseph smiled beatifically. She had been thinking about this sort of scene for some time and at last she had had the courage to put herself first – calmly and without a fuss. She felt exhilarated. 'There's the iron – the board's in the cupboard. I'm off. Have a good day, dear.'

She turned to Jon, who was stuffing the remnants of a slice of toast into his mouth and trying not to laugh.

'Jon? If you want a lift to the bus stop, you'll have to come now. I don't want to be late for registration.'

Jon grabbed his rugby kit and school bag and grinned. He had a feeling his dad was finding it hard to accept that Mum was heading into the big wide world.

'Bye, Dad!' he called.

His father, clutching a shirt and viewing the iron with the same degree of suspicion as he would greet a boa constrictor, said nothing. It's difficult to talk when you are in a state of advanced shock.

Chapter Eight

Figuratively Speaking

Next door, Jemma Farrant was trying to work out how many calories there were in a blueberry and mango yogurt and one slice of crispbread (no butter, small smear of

Marmite). It wasn't easy because on one side her father was holding forth about the importance of the coming school year and the necessity for hard work and the production of superior coursework, and on the other her mother was getting very worked up about Jemma's uneaten Weetabix.

'Jemma, love, don't you feel well?' she asked, anxiety creasing her forehead.

'I'm fine, Mum,' sighed Jemma.

'You must eat to keep your strength up,' insisted her mother. 'You've got a busy term ahead. Come on now, petal.'

'Mum, I've told you, I'm on a diet. I've had a yogurt and I'm not hungry. And don't call me petal,' retorted Jemma.

'But darling, it's so silly to diet at your age – you need all your strength. And besides, you're not fat, not at all.'

Jemma said nothing.

'Andrew, say something,' said Claire, turning to her husband.

'Something,' said Jemma's dad.

Chapter Nine

Agony Mother

Ginny Gee waved Chelsea off to school, phoned the office and said she had a touch of Spanish tummy and would be in tomorrow and flopped into an armchair. How come, she thought, her daughter could throw on a cheap skirt and cropped top from the market, wield an eyeliner for five seconds and look like something out of the centrefold of *Style Hi!* while she, Ginny Gee, Agony Aunt and Columnist, was beginning to look saggy and baggy even when dressed in Chic Elite designer clothes?

She poured herself a large mug of coffee and started thinking. Things were not looking good. For one thing, that Barclaycard bill had only been the tip of the iceberg. She knew full well that within a few days MasterCard would be requesting money, the building society would feel obliged to remind her that the last mortgage payment was overdue, and it seemed highly likely that the exhaust would fall off her car the moment she tried to drive it.

The fact was, she loved spending money. And the older she got, the more she loved it. Shopping, whether for clothes or books or simply a new jug for the kitchen, was to her like aspirin to a headache; an effective, if only temporary, relief from the worries and problems of every-day life.

The trouble was that, although she wouldn't admit it to anyone, she wasn't enjoying work as much as she used to. Since winning the Regional Feature Writer of the Year Award, everyone at the paper had expected her to be even more sparkling and thrusting and lively than before and frankly, it was all getting a bit much. The holiday had been great but for the first time ever, she had had no desire to get back to work. In the past she would never have pretended to be ill – in fact, in the past she went to work even when she really was ill.

Barry had been really off with her since yesterday. Oh, she knew she shouldn't really have bought all those clothes but she had to do something to keep her spirits up. She hated getting older, putting on weight and coping with those ghastly hot flushes that made her look like a beetroot and feel like a cauldron of curry. The odd new skirt or pair of shoes made all the difference. And now it seemed she couldn't even have those.

Still, moping wouldn't do any good. She'd phone Ruth Turnbull. Ruth would be a good source of money saving tips – she had had two years of being hard up before Peter sold the family home – and she had managed. Besides, it was time they had a natter. She refilled her coffee cup and went to the telephone. At least it was only a local call, she told herself. And a good gossip was worth its weight in gold.

Chapter Ten

Mum in Decline

Laura was just going out of the front door when the phone rang. Perhaps it was Jon, she thought, desperate to see her after so long. She grabbed it on the second ring. 'Leehampton 870775, Laura Turnbull speaking.'

It wasn't Jon.

'Oh, hi, Mrs Gee – yes great, thanks. I'll call Mum for you.' Laura yelled up the stairs. 'Mum, it's Chelsea's mum for you.'

Silence.

'MUM! Telephone!'

Laura galloped up the stairs two at a time and hammered on the bathroom door.

There was the inimitable sound of heaving.

'Are you OK, Mum?'

'No, I am not flaming well OK!' groaned Ruth. 'Go away.'

Laura pounded back down the stairs.

'Mum's not feeling too good, Mrs Gee – she says she'll call you back. Pardon? OK, I tell her you'll call again later.'

Laura hung up and hesitated. She wanted to dash to the bus stop in case she caught a sight of Jon on the Bellborough bus. On the other hand, she supposed she ought to stay and see if Mum was all right.

At that moment, Ruth Turnbull appeared at the top of the stairs. Her face was the colour of cement and judging from the way she was clutching the banister, her sense of balance was not up to much either.

'Mum, you look awful!' said Laura.

'Oh thanks,' said Ruth dryly. 'I don't exactly feel like a million dollars. I suppose it's just something I ate. Nothing to worry about – I'll be fine.'

'Oh good. Well, I'm off. See ya,' and with that she crashed through the front door with all the delicacy of a stampeding water buffalo.

So much, thought Ruth, for tender loving care.

Chapter Eleven

Fame on the Menu

'It's arrived!' said Barry excitedly, waving an envelope in Ginny's face. 'Hey, why are you here? Shouldn't you be at work?'

'No, not till tomorrow,' said Ginny dismissively. 'Anyway, what's come?'

'My acceptance for *Superchef*! It says, *Please attend Television Centre at 9.00 a.m. on November 1st for recording.* I did it, Ginny – I'm in the first round!'

'That's nice,' said Ginny, trying to muster up some enthusiasm. 'Do they pay you?'

'Well no, not unless I win it – then there's a £10,000 prize and all sorts of kitchen gadgetry and the chance to have your recipes published and . . .'

'So I suppose we can forget the possibility of your looking for a proper job, you know, the sort that pays money at the end of each month,' she said sarcastically.

'Oh for Pete's sake, Ginny, can't you show a bit of enthusiasm? I always back you when you're on those phone-ins; I read every damned word you write. Can't you at least pretend to care?'

'Sorry,' said Ginny.

'And as it happens, I think within a few days I could be set up with a nice little earner,' he added.

Ginny brightened visibly.

'That's great – what is it? Where?'

'Well . . .' began Barry.

'And is there a pension?' Ginny interrupted. 'How much will you be getting? Will there be a company car?'

Ah, thought Barry. He knew his idea was a good one; now all he had to do was convince the bank manager, make a few basic purchases and he was in business. Then Ginny would be thrilled. She wouldn't mind about pensions and stuff, would she?

'Go on,' encouraged Ginny. 'Tell me – what is the job?'

'Wait and see,' he said, reasoning that there was no point having a row before you had to.

Chapter Twelve

New Beginnings

Jon sat on the school bus wishing this year would fly past. It wasn't that he hated Bellborough Court; simply that he couldn't wait for his GCSEs to be over and to start his A-level art and design course at Lee Hill. He wished he was there now; Rob had said that the school was doing a production of *Oliver!* at Christmas – designing the set for that would be amazing. The workhouse, the riverside taverns, the rooftop chase at the end – already his mind was sketching out stage layouts and imagining how he would light it. The thing was, all his mental pictures had Sumitha standing centre stage. Every time he sketched, it was her face that stared back out at him. He wondered how he could get to see her again – perhaps she would be at The Stomping Ground on Saturday? But then again, maybe not – he remembered her saying that her father was anti-clubbing and the only way she got there last time was by pretending she was going somewhere else. Still, it might be worth giving it a go.

As the bus turned into the school gates there was a commotion. Horns honked, and Jim, the bus driver who was normally as laid back as a comatose tortoise, swore violently and slammed on the brakes.

'Bloody rich kids,' he muttered under his breath. Jon peered through the misted up window.

'What's going on?' he asked the guy in front.

'Only Bilu Chakrabarti showing off again,' said his mate, grinning. 'Looks like he's got a flash new car. I guess the whole school will get to hear about it by lunch time.'

Jon grimaced. Bilu was not known for his modesty. Captain of the cricket team, vice-captain of the debating team and the school high diving champion, he was one of those guys for whom everything seemed to turn to gold. Half the girls in the school professed to be madly in love with him – and yet most of the boys weren't that keen on him. Somehow Jon got the idea that fast cars and designer clothes meant more to Bilu than people.

But Jon had more important things on his mind than Bilu. He'd just had a brilliant idea for a cartoon and had to get it down on paper before assembly.

Chapter Thirteen

New Friends

Meanwhile, Jon's mother was heading into the main hall of Leehampton College of Further Education with some-what less enthusiasm than her son. What was she doing here? she asked herself, gazing around the crowded room. Anona was conscious that she was old enough to be mother to most of the students here, and despite having taken an hour to dress that morning, felt absurdly out of place in her smart skirt and lacy knit top. Perhaps Henry was right after all; maybe she was just acting on some stupid, mid-life whim. Maybe she should have stuck with flower arranging.

'Hi there, you new here too?' She turned to find a tall fair-haired guy grinning at her and waving a piece of paper. 'I'm looking for Interior Design Stage One registration – don't know where that would be, do you?'

Anona felt a surge of relief. 'That's what I'm doing, too,' she said. 'I think it's over that way.' She pointed across the room to where a large black sign hung askew on a pillar, the letters '*Des–*' just visible.

'Great – let's saunter over then,' he said. 'I'm Vernon, by the way.' He held out a hand.

'I'm Anona – Anona Joseph,' Anona replied. 'Have you done this sort of thing before?' He may not be as old as me, thought Anona, but at least he's over twenty-five.

'No way,' said Vernon, laughing, as they joined the queue for registration. 'I was made redundant back in the summer and rather than sit around waiting for some job to drop into my lap I reckoned this was the time to do something I've always wanted to have a go at. So here I am. I reckon it's going to be fun. It'll be a challenge, that's for sure.'

Yes, thought Anona, and that's what I need. For once, I can do something just for me.

Chapter Fourteen

Baby Blues

At the same time, Mrs Farrant was sitting at the kitchen table, weeping on to an Oatmeal HobNob. The twins had started nursery full time today and there was no one left at home. The house was so quiet she could hear all the clocks ticking. She had waxed the kitchen floor, changed the sheets on Jemma's bed and made a cheese and onion flan – and it was still only eleven o'clock. What was she going to do until three p.m. when she could fetch the twins and Sam? And what was she going to do tomorrow?

As if by telepathy, the phone rang. It was Mrs Banerji. She sounded harassed.

'Claire, I am in need of help. Can you come down to the Centre now? Please? Just for a couple of hours. Ellie, who runs our crèche, has been sent home sick and I'm stuck here with eight under-threes and a class full of women trying to learn English. You know I'm useless with little kids. Please, Claire.'

'I'm on my way,' said Claire.

The thought of a morning spent with a clutch of toddlers put a spring in her step as she hurried out.

Chapter Fifteen

Why Me? Why Now?

'Leehampton 870 . . . Oh, hi Ginny.' Ruth closed her eyes. Much as she liked her zany friend, right now she didn't want to talk to anybody.

'Hi, Roo, are you feeling better?' gabbled Ginny.

'Well, not really, I . . .' began Ruth wearily.

'Oh good. Well, the thing is, all hell's been let loose here and I really need to talk before I go off my trolley. Can I come round for a coffee? I phoned the office and told them I'm sick.'

You're sick? thought Ruth. I think I might die any minute.

'Ruth?' Ginny's voice was insistent. 'You still there?'

'Yes,' sighed Ruth, willing her undisciplined stomach to stay still for five seconds. 'Yes, I'm still here.'

'Oh fine,' said Ginny. 'So, I'll come round in about ten minutes – I really do need some advice.'

Ruth dragged herself into the kitchen and flopped down at the table. Perhaps she'd feel better if she ate something. She half-heartedly made some toast, spread it with Marmite and nibbled the edge. Her stomach disapproved. Forcibly. Ruth rushed to the bathroom.

Chapter Sixteen

Stage Directions

While Laura's mum was parting company with her breakfast, her daughter, along with rest of Year Ten, was listening to Mr Todd's start-of-year pep talk in assembly. Listening is perhaps an overstatement; since Toddy said the same thing, more or less, every year you only needed to home in on the essentials. So it wasn't until the word *Oliver!* hit her consciousness that she began to pay attention.

'I shall be pinning up audition lists at break time,' intoned Mr Todd, beaming at the assembled throng. 'And do all take part – if you don't want to perform, then think about lighting, props, programme design – remember, boys and girls . . .'

'It's the taking part that matters,' mouthed two hundred and fifty pupils silently. It was one of Toddy's pet phrases.

AUDITION LISTS FOR OLIVER!

Role	Name
Oliver	Dougie Glass
	James Gill
Mr Bumble	Robert Goodwin
	Ian Morris

Nancy	?

Bill Sykes	Ben Grantley
	Rob Antell
	Edward Stammers

| Artful Dodger | Sumitha Banerji |
| | Jo Bond |

Fagin	Tim Pryor
	Russell Markstein
	Grant Nisbet

Those wishing to form the chorus i.e. orphan boys, Fagin's crew, tavern girls, street sellers, etc. should sign below.

Laura had been doing a lot of thinking on the topic of *Oliver!* If she could get a starring role, and if she could somehow wangle things so that Jon came along to watch, she could wow him with her charisma and he would fall blindly in love with her. The trouble was, Laura couldn't sing and hated dancing. But the plan was too good to discard without some further deep thought on the matter.

And so it was that Laura had her brilliant idea.

'Hey, look, Chelsea,' called Jemma at break time. 'Rob's auditioning for the part of Bill Sykes. You didn't say.'

Because he didn't tell me, thought Chelsea ruefully, peering at the list of names.

'I wonder who'll be Nancy?' said Laura wickedly. 'Think, all that canoodling and fluttering of eyelashes. Maybe,' she added, 'I should try for the part.'

'You can't sing,' snapped Chelsea who couldn't either.

'That is true,' agreed Laura. 'Well, I wonder who will get the part? I bet Mandy Fincham will have a go – she's got a voice to die for. And she'd be a perfect Nancy – all that tossing of hair and showing of thigh.'

Chelsea felt close to tears. Mandy Fincham oozed confidence from every pore and when she perched on a desktop, crossed her legs, flicked back that gorgeous blond hair and smiled her dazzling toothpaste-ad smile, rugby lads went weak at the knees. There was nothing for it; much as Chelsea loathed amateur dramatics, she would have to audition. It was that, or dying of a broken heart. Reluctantly, she signed her name.

Chapter Seventeen

A Pregnant Pause

Ruth Turnbull opened the door to find Ginny dressed in a scarlet and cinnamon suit which was a little loud at the

best of times and definitely a threat to Ruth in her weak-
ened state of health.

'Hi, Ruth, lovely to see you,' she said, breezing into the
hallway. 'My God, you look like death! Have you got this
bug that's going around?'

'Mmm,' said Ruth non-commitally. 'Anyway, what's up
with you – you said you needed advice. Oh, by the way,
could you put the kettle on – kitchens and me are not
getting on awfully well right now.'

Ginny went through to the kitchen, her gold stiletto
sandals clicking on the quarry tiles, and filled the kettle,
Ruth followed her and leaned on the doorpost.

'It's money,' said Ginny shortly. 'The plain fact of the
matter is, we don't have enough of it.'

Gosh, I do feel ill, thought Ruth.

'Oh dear,' she muttered, in what she hoped were interested tones. Frankly, she wasn't in the mood for anyone's
problems but her own right now.

'Barry says it's my fault for spending too much and I
must cut back,' continued Ginny. 'Which is a bit much,
since I'm the one doing all the earning. Anyway, since you
were always hard up when Peter left, I thought you'd
know how I could make some savings. You always have
life well under control, despite everything.'

Ruth burst into tears.

'Oh, Ruth, I didn't mean – I mean, when I said you are
always hard up, what I meant was . . .'

'No, no, it's all right,' sniffed Ruth, fumbling for a tissue in her dressing gown pocket. 'It's not that. Oh, I might as well tell you. But don't breathe a word to a living soul. Promise?'

'Cross my heart and hope to die, as we used to say as kids,' said Ginny. 'But what is it? What's wrong?' Surely Melvyn hasn't upped and left her? she thought.

'I'm – well, you see – oh no, I think I'm going to be sick again.' And with that she fled to the loo.

Oh my heavens, thought Ginny. Not that. She's not. She can't be. She could be.

Ruth returned.

'Ruth, you're not – I mean, being sick and every-thing – ?'

Ruth nodded.

'Yes,' she said. 'I am. I'm pregnant.'

Ginny stared, open-mouthed. 'Oh no!' she breathed. 'Oh knickers. That is to say, well – I mean – congratulations.'

'I think,' said Ruth wryly, 'that the "Oh no" and "Oh knickers" were more appropriate.'

'But how did it happen?' asked Ginny.

Ruth laughed despite herself. 'That's rich, coming from you – agony aunt to the Young and Uninformed,' she said. 'It happened in pretty much the usual way.'

'But I mean – weren't you taking precautions?'

'Yes, of course – I had a cap. Except I sometimes forgot to use it. Stupid, eh?'

'What does Melvyn say?' asked Ginny, who was grappling with a whole range of emotions like 'what must

40

it be like to have a baby at forty-two?' and 'thank heavens it's not me' to 'I wish it was me' and 'I'll buy it a pair of those dinky little socks with frills on.'

Ruth chewed her lip. 'I haven't told him,' she admitted. 'Or Laura.'

'Well,' said Ginny, adopting her Very Together Agony Aunt voice, 'you can't put it off any longer. You are going to have to tell them both.'

'I know,' said Ruth. 'But, Ginny, – how can I cope with a baby now? I mean, I'm forty-two, for heaven's sake. All that getting up in the night and stuff. And what if Melvyn runs a mile when he hears? What then?'

'Then you would be well shot of him,' said Ginny briskly. 'But my guess is he will be over the moon.' Ginny surveyed her friend quizzically. 'How do you feel about it all – really?'

'Well,' said Ruth, 'half of me is totally gobsmacked, a quarter is scared silly and the other quarter is quite pleased.' She took a tentative sip of coffee. She was beginning to feel better. Then she remembered. 'The hardest bit,' said Ruth ominously, 'will be telling Laura. That won't be easy.'

Too right, thought Ginny. But she said nothing.

Chapter Eighteen

Stormy Waters

The first week of the autumn term proved to be more eventful than any of them could have imagined that first morning.

On Monday evening, Chelsea's parents had a row. The sort of shouting, slamming doors, stamping up and down stairs sort of row that made any thoughts of memorising the effects of sunlight on plants quite impossible.

'What on earth's going on?' shouted Chelsea as her mother chucked a telephone directory at the sitting room door.

'Ask your father!' snapped Ginny, and flounced into the kitchen.

'Dad?' queried Chelsea poking her head round the door. 'Dad? What's up with you two?'

'Ask your mother!' muttered her father morosely.

She shrugged and returned to her room to grapple with photosynthesis. Ten minutes later, the arguing started again.

'What do you mean, you spent it?' shouted her father.

'Well, I thought . . .' she heard her mum say.

'No you didn't think at all,' snapped her father. 'Are you going nuts or something? I suppose it's your age. At least I'm trying to find a solution to our problems. You just go leaping into Chanel and make them ten times worse.'

'Oh, go and boil your head!' said Mrs Gee.

'Mum! Dad! Will you just stop it!' yelled Chelsea. She wasn't used to her parents arguing like this and she didn't like it.

Just then the doorbell rang.

No one answered it. It rang again.

'I'll get it,' sighed Chelsea.

Rob stood on the doorstep, clutching a sheaf of paper. Chelsea's stomach performed a perfect double somersault.

'Hi, Chelsea,' he said, 'is your mum in?' Before Chelsea could reply, Ginny came to the door.

'No, I'm not, I'm going out and don't be surprised if I don't come back!' Her mother barged past the two astonished kids, her lips set in a tight line.

'Mu-umm!' muttered Chelsea as her mother pushed past them, climbed into the car (showing, Chelsea thought, a rather unnecessary amount of thigh), revved the engine and drove off.

'Er, sorry about that,' Chelsea said, trying a grin. 'Mental or what?'

'Don't worry,' said Rob, 'my mum does it all the time. Dad says it's her age – personally I think it's her brain!'

Chelsea grinned. 'Do you want to come in and have a coffee?' she said.

Rob remembered how he felt when his mum burst into tears on the top of a number 11 bus in full view of six of his mates.

'Why not?' he said. 'We sane guys have got to close ranks.'

I *do* love him, thought Chelsea.

43

Chapter Nineteen
Melvyn Takes to Cloud Nine

On Tuesday, Mrs Turnbull telephoned Melvyn at the office.

'I need to see you. Now,' said Ruth.

'I'll be over tonight around seven,' said Melvyn, peering distractedly at his computer screen.

'No. Now!' said Ruth. And burst into tears.

'I'm on my way,' said Melvyn, gently.

'Burst water pipes,' he muttered to his boss, as he picked up his jacket and headed out of the office. 'Got to sort a plumber.'

What shall I say? thought Ruth. How shall I put it? 'Hi Melvyn, you're going to be a father?' No, that's too blunt. 'Well, hello darling, I've some great news.' No, that's wrong. He'll run a mile, I know he will.

The bell rang.

Now just take it calmly, Laura's mum told herself. She opened the door.

'What's wrong, love?' asked Melvyn taking her arm and leading her through to the sitting room.

'I'm pregnant,' gulped Ruth. So much for tact and diplomacy, she thought.

Melvyn's jaw dropped open and he stared at her in wide-eyed amazement.

'You're what?'

I knew he'd be furious, thought Ruth miserably.

'I know, I know, I'm sorry, it's stupid, I . . .'

'Hang on, hang on. Just say it again. Tell me again.'

'I'm going to have a baby. Your baby,' said Ruth, just in case he was tempted to think this whole procreation business was purely down to her.

Melvyn's face creased into one enormous grin and he flung his arms round Ruth, lifted her off her feet and swung her round.

'That's wonderful – a baby! Us! Oh, that's just incredible!' he cried, clasping his hands to his head.

Ruth bit her lip. 'Are you sure it's wonderful? I mean, we can't really afford it, can we? And aren't I too old? What are we going to do?'

'I couldn't be more thrilled,' said Melvyn. 'I'm thirty-five and I'm dying to be a father – thought it might never happen to me. And yes, we can and we will afford it. As for what we are going to do, I am going to move in with you and start taking proper care of you.'

Ruth stared at him. She hadn't thought as far as domestic arrangements. She knew one person who would not approve of that.

'There is just one thing,' ventured Ruth.

'What's that?' asked Melvyn.

'Laura,' said Ruth. 'I haven't told her yet.'

Chapter Twenty

The Lure of the Footlights

'So I am pleased to announce that Rob Antell will play Bill Sykes, Sumitha Banerji will be the Artful Dodger and . . .'

Chelsea held her breath.

'Mandy Fincham has got the part of Nancy.' Mr Horage beamed round the hall.

Typical, thought Chelsea.

'Mandy was brilliant, wasn't she?' enthused Rob, when they broke for refreshments. 'She's going to be great to act with.'

Chelsea wanted to cry. Just when she thought things were beginning to look good between her and Rob. Perhaps her mum had the right idea after all. Maybe you had to be over the top to get anywhere. Her mum seemed to get noticed wherever she went – she didn't let silly inhibitions hold her back. Perhaps pushing yourself into the limelight was the only way. She would have to work on it. One thing she was sure of; she was not about to lose Rob to that cow Mandy Fincham.

While Chelsea was wondering whether she could put cyanide in Mandy Fincham's crisps, Mr Horage was dishing out understudy parts.

'And Jemma Farrant, I'd like you to understudy the part of Nancy,' he announced.

'But I can't,' she protested. 'I mean . . .'

'Jemma, you can,' he said. 'You have a lovely voice and an excellent memory for lines. I can't think why you didn't go for a major part. Anyway, you'll be a great asset to the chorus and fill in for Mandy if the need arises.'

'Oh do it, Jemma,' muttered Mandy Fincham. 'You won't be needed because no way am I missing this opportunity – not even if bubonic plague strikes!'

'Oh, all right, then,' said Jemma. Anything for a quiet life.

'Now then,' continued Mr Horage, scanning his clipboard. 'I think that's most of the roles filled. I need a few more girls for the chorus – street sellers, tavern girls, that sort of thing. Any volunteers?'

'I will, sir,' called Chelsea. If she couldn't star opposite Rob, she'd make damn sure she was on stage with a beady eye on the two of them as often as possible.

A few others put up their hands. Mr Horage looked pleasantly surprised. 'Great – well, thank you all for that.'

'And Laura Turnbull has volunteered to be in charge of publicity – posters, programmes, that sort of thing,' he concluded. 'Thank you all for coming – first rehearsal next Monday after school.'

'What's with this publicity lark?' Chelsea asked Laura as they walked to the bus stop. 'Sounds like hard work to me having to design posters and stuff and anyway, I thought writing was your thing . . . hang on a minute. I get it.' Chelsea turned to her friend and grinned. 'You're going to get Jon to help you, aren't you? Appeal to his male ego? Ask his advice?'

'So what if I am?' asked Laura defensively, annoyed at her brilliant plan being sussed so quickly. 'He's very good at that sort of thing.'

I'm sure that's not the only thing you'd like him to be good at, thought Chelsea.

Chapter Twenty-One

Schemes and Dreams

Mrs Banerji was delighted when her daughter announced that she had a major part in the school musical. It would, she thought, give her something other than Bilu to think about. She knew Rajiv thought that Bilu would be an influence for good on his daughter, but Chitrita wasn't so sure. He had delightful manners, good social graces and of course, his family were very well respected. But there was something that made her uneasy.

Sumitha was bending over backwards to be charming. She helped her mother dish up supper and asked her father whether he had had a good day at the hospital. She even helped her young brother, Sandeep, make a mask from the back of his cereal packet and managed to refrain from yelling at him when he put lilac felt tip on her shirt collar.

'What time tomorrow does Bilu arrive?' asked Mr Banerji.

'Six o'clock,' said Sumitha at once. 'He's collecting his car from the headmaster's house and coming straight over.'

'Such a personable boy,' murmured Rajiv.

Strike while the iron is hot, thought Sumitha.

'Dad, would you mind if I took Bilu along to The Stomping Ground on Saturday night?' She held her breath.

Ah, thought Sumitha's mother – so that was what all this helpfulness has been about.

'That club place?' queried her father with a frown. 'The one you went to without my permission?'

'Yes, but I wouldn't do that again, I've learned my lesson,' said Sumitha quickly, putting on what she hoped was a penitent expression. 'That's why I'm asking. It'll be fine – Bilu will look after me,' she added.

'Well,' said her father doubtfully, 'I am not sure what his family would think of my allowing my daughter in such a place. Bilu has been brought up with high ideals, you know.'

'Which is why I would be fine with him,' ventured Sumitha. 'We could ask him.'

'All right,' agreed her father 'But I think you will find he will be against it. And if he is, that is the end of the matter.'

'Yes, Dad,' said Sumitha meekly. She was pretty sure she was home and dry.

While Sumitha was busy buttering up her father, Jemma was being buttered up by her mum.

'Your father's playing in the Golf Club One Day Tournament on Sunday and I thought it would be a lovely idea if we all went along,' said Mrs Farrant. 'They're having a family day with the pool open, and games for the little ones – won't that be fun?'

'Hilarious,' muttered Jemma, flicking through her new *Yell!* magazine. 'Oh Mum, do I have to?'

'Well, of course, darling. We've only just joined the club and it will be a good opportunity for you to make some nice friends. There are some very important people at that club,' she added proudly, as if she had personally placed them all there.

Jemma sighed. 'It'll be sooo boring – and I've got loads of homework,' she said in a sudden flash of inspiration.

'Well, then, you had better do that on Saturday evening instead of going to the club, hadn't you?' said her mother, with a smile.

'OK, I'll come.' Jemma sighed. 'If I must.'

'That's it, petal – you'll enjoy it once you're there. Shall I iron that pretty little skirt with the seagulls on it?'

'NO!' cried Jemma. '*I'll* choose something – OK?'

Claire Farrant sighed as Jemma retreated to her room. Jemma was growing up and even she couldn't deny it any longer. She didn't want her mother fussing over her – indeed, sometimes Claire felt as though no one wanted her any more. Sam was almost eight and interested only in football and Xbox and now that the twins were at full-time nursery, the days seemed very long.

It had been great at the crèche. Surrounded by all those little ones, doing finger painting and playing in the sand had reminded her of the days when Jemma was little. And lovable. And biddable. But Ellie, the regular girl, had got over her bug and was back in full swing. Where do I go from here? thought Claire.

Similar thoughts were weighing heavily on Henry Joseph's mind that morning. He had just shown a couple barely out of their teens round one of the new starter homes on the Ibstock estate, and become increasingly depressed as he listened to their excited chatter. It reminded him of when he and Anona got married, and lived in that poky little flat at the top of an old Victorian house. But they had thought it was paradise.

He had had such hopes, such aspirations. Oh, he knew that by many people's standards he had done well – senior member of a respected firm of estate agents, nice house on Billing Hill, son at private school. But what was it all for? What did it mean? And if he died tomorrow, what mark would he have left on the world?

Even the hopes he had cherished for Jon seemed to be coming to nothing. Once Henry realised that his own career was never going to hit the heights, he'd hung all his hopes on being the father of Jon Joseph, renowned barrister. This art school idea of his was, Henry feared, no mere flash in the pan. The lad spent all his spare time sketching and painting and designing and now his mother was launching herself into this design lark, they would probably both be in huddles talking about Rembrandt and Andy Warhol and he'd feel left out.

He couldn't bear the thought of being shut out of Jon's life. He had always assumed he and Anona would have a whole brood of kids but it hadn't worked out like that. He had to hang on to Jon. He had to think of some way of strengthening the bond, of remaining a big part of his life.

As it turned out, fate was due to give him a helping hand.

Chapter Twenty-Two

In at the Deep End

By Saturday afternoon, Mrs Turnbull knew she couldn't put it off any longer. Laura was going out to The Stomping Ground for the evening and Melvyn was coming for Sunday lunch the following day. If she didn't tell her the news now, she wouldn't get a chance and

Melvyn was in such a state of excitement that he would be bound to let something slip and that would be a recipe for disaster.

She tapped on Laura's bedroom door.

'Can I come in, love?' she asked.

A muffled grunt emitted from the other side.

Laura, her ginger hair scooped back in a hair band, was sitting in front of her dressing table mirror, frowning, open-mouthed, and wielding an eyeliner pencil.

'Are you OK now?' Laura enquired. Her mother had been sick again that morning – but then, she'd been out with Mrs Gee the evening before, so they had probably been drinking vast quantities of wine. She couldn't be properly ill because she was always fine by the time Laura got home from school.

'Well, not really, that is . . .' Oh gosh, this isn't going to be easy, thought Mrs Turnbull, flopping down on Laura's bed and running her fingers through her hair. Where do I begin?

'What is it? You're not *still* ill, are you?' said Laura accusingly.

'No. Yes. Well, sort of,' began her mother, 'the thing is . . .'

'Oh my God,' interrupted Laura, dropping her eyeliner pencil on the floor and turning to her mother. 'You've got one of those awful diseases, haven't you? That's why you keep throwing up. You've been given weeks to live, and I'm going to be an orphan – oh my . . .'

'NO! No, of course I haven't. Don't be daft – there's nothing wrong with me. Well, not like that anyway,' said Mrs Turnbull. 'The thing is – well, actually –' she took a deep breath, 'I'm pregnant.'

Laura stared at her mother in disbelief.

'You're – WHAT?' she exclaimed.

'I'm going to have a baby,' said her mother, smiling in what she hoped was a confident and relaxed manner. 'Sometime early March, I guess.'

'A baby – YOU? But you can't – I mean – that's disgusting!' shouted Laura, knocking over a pot of foundation in her fury. 'You – at your age – having a baby! Oh Mum, how could you?' Laura's eyes filled with angry tears. 'I suppose that jerk Melvyn is responsible?'

'Well, yes, he did have something to do with it,' said Ruth wryly. 'Who do you think?'

'But – that's disgusting!' she cried. 'You'll have to get rid of it!'

'LAURA!' Ruth exploded. 'That's a terrible, terrible thing to say. I want – we want – this baby.' Yes, she thought in surprise. Yes, I really do. She took a deep breath. 'I admit, it took me by surprise at first, but now I'm delighted. And when you get used to the idea, you'll be thrilled too. Just think, a little brother or sister.'

'But what do you want a baby for?' asked Laura. 'You've got me.'

Her mother pulled Laura to her. 'Look, love, it won't make a single difference to the way I feel about you, if

54

that's what's worrying you. I love you to bits and I always will – no baby in the world is going to alter that.'

'God, what will my friends say?' cried Laura, wriggling free of her mother's embrace. 'What will your friends say – Chelsea's mum will be disgusted.'

'Actually, she's being very supportive,' began Ruth.

'Oh I see – so you told her before you own daughter! See how much you care.'

'I only told her because she was here and I was sick and she guessed,' sighed Ruth. 'No one else knows – except Melvyn, of course.'

'So you haven't told Dad?' demanded Laura.

'No, no of course not. Not yet,' said Ruth.

'Well, I should think he will be devastated,' shouted Laura. 'His own wife – with that jerk –'

'Laura, listen. I am not Dad's wife any more as you know full well. Dad and I are not a couple; we're divorced. What he does is no business of mine, and what I choose to do is no concern of his. And you are going to have to learn to accept that fact.'

Laura burst into hot tears. 'You're ruining my entire life, you know that, don't you? First of all you dump Dad, then you go around with someone half your age . . .'

Ruth sighed. 'Seven years younger than me, actually – and I didn't dump Dad, as you put it. He met someone else.'

Her daughter was in no mood to listen to reason.

'. . . and then you get pregnant. You'll be puking all

over the place and then you'll get all fat and gross and everyone will know what you've been doing. I HATE YOU!'

She stormed into the bathroom and slammed the door. A crack appeared on the landing ceiling. Ruth sat on the bed wondering whether entering the minefield called motherhood for a second time was such a good idea after all.

'We'll talk about it some more tomorrow – Melvyn's coming for lunch,' ventured Ruth through the keyhole.

'Then I shall be out,' shouted Laura. 'I have no intention of being in the same room as that pervert.'

Ten minutes later, the telephone rang. It was Chelsea.

'Hi, Mrs Turnbull, can I have a word with Laura, please?'

Ruth called up the stairs. 'Laura, it's Chelsea for you.'

A red-eyed Laura appeared at the top of the stairs.

'I can't talk to anyone,' she sniffed. 'I'm in shock.'

'Um, Chelsea, Laura's a little bit tied up right now . . . yes, tonight? All right, seven-thirty. Who? Oh, all right. Yes, yes I'll tell her. Bye, Chelsea.'

'Mrs Gee will pick you up at seven-thirty,' said Laura's mum. 'So you had better smarten up pretty sharpish and put a smile on your face.'

'I don't think,' said Laura dramatically, 'that I shall ever smile again.'

Laura turned to go into her bedroom.

56

'Oh and Chelsea said . . .'

The door slammed. Oh forget it, thought Ruth. What's the point of my making an effort when she's in this frame of mind? I don't suppose it matters whether she knows Jon someone or other is going or not.

At seven-twenty, Mrs Gee rang the Turnbulls' front door bell.

'Sorry we're early, but is Laura ready?' she asked when Ruth opened the door. Her friend was looking markedly less pallid than when she last saw her.

'Yes I am,' Laura thundered downstairs, grabbed her bag and marched out of the house without saying a word.

'I take it,' mouthed Ginny to Ruth, 'Madam now knows of the new arrival.'

Ruth nodded.

'I won't ask how she took it,' said Ginny.

Chapter Twenty-Three

Introducing Bilu

Laura sat silently staring out of the car window all the way into town. Since her friends usually found it hard to get a word in edgeways when she was around, this was somewhat noticeable. Normally, Chelsea's mum would have filled any awkward silences with a stream of bright chat but she was unusually subdued as well. I guess there's a first time for everything, thought Chelsea.

In fact, Mrs Gee was brooding on just what her husband was up to. He had left the house at eight thirty that morning, and when she had asked where he was off to, he had merely tapped the side of his nose and said, 'Ask no questions, hear no lies,' and departed.

And he still wasn't back.

She just hoped it was a job interview, but she didn't think it was likely on a Saturday.

'I can't wait to meet Bilu,' Chelsea said, trying to break the silence and wondering just what had got into Laura. She had thought she would be over the moon at the thought of seeing Jon again.

'Mmm,' muttered Laura. It'll cry all night and puke all day, she thought.

'Is Rob going to be there tonight?' Jemma asked Chelsea.

'Yes,' said Chelsea, with a dreamy smile on her lips. 'I told you, he's coming with . . .'

'Now listen,' interrupted Chelsea's mum, pulling up outside The Stomping Ground, 'I'll meet you at eleven o'clock sharp. I don't want to be kept waiting.'

During those first awkward moments when you want to look as though you are with a guy even if you are not, Jemma and Chelsea grabbed a corner table and got some

Cokes. Laura sat moodily stirring her drink with a straw and planning various horrible deaths for Melvyn.

Just as she had got to the bit where Melvyn fell into a water butt and drowned, Rob turned up. Chelsea spotted him lurking by the door, and remembering her vow to go for it, she dashed over, planted a kiss on his lips and said 'Hi, darling'. Rob turned an interesting shade resembling a lobster and scanned the room anxiously.

'Come on, we're over there in the corner,' urged Chelsea, slipping her arm through Rob's and pulling him across the floor.

There was no sign of Jon but Chelsea thought it wiser not to say anything. Laura seemed moody enough without making things worse.

Laura's ponderings about the merits of poisoning by toadstool over death by electrocution were interrupted by the arrival of Sumitha and Bilu.

'Hi everyone, this is Bilu,' said Sumitha, as proudly as if she had hand-crafted him herself.

'Well, hi there,' said Bilu, flashing a detergent white grin at them all. 'How are you doing?'

'Hi,' they chorused. He was tall, lean and wore immaculately cut jeans that definitely did not come from a market stall. His dark hair curled into the nape of his neck without any of those straggly bits that lesser mortals get and his broad smile revealed a set of even teeth. His carefully managed casual pose against the wall suggested that he knew he was dynamite.

Nice legs, thought Chelsea.

Great bum, thought Jemma.

How could my mother do it to me? thought Laura.

'So this is the infamous Stomping Ground,' said Bilu, surveying the dance floor. 'What are you drinking, Sumitha?'

'Coke, please,' she said breathlessly, aware that all her friends were pretty impressed.

Bilu laughed. 'Yes, I suppose on teenyboppers' night that's all we're going to get, isn't it? Bye bye Bacardi.'

Sumitha looked surprised. 'You don't drink, do you?'

'Now what made you think that, my little one,' said Bilu in patronising tones.

'Well, Dad said that Bengali boys . . .' began Sumitha.

'Oh, your dad. Anyway,' interrupted Bilu, 'let's show them how it's done,' and he whirled Sumitha on to the dance floor.

'What do you think?' asked Jemma, after they had disappeared.

'He's OK,' said Chelsea, grudgingly. 'If you like that sort of thing.'

'Which I don't,' said Rob shortly, looking at the door. Oh whoopee, thought Chelsea, he's jealous.

'You're nicer,' she whispered to Rob. Rob swallowed and said, 'I'll just go and get some crisps.'

'Bilu's a bit big for his boots, if you ask me,' said Jemma. 'What do you reckon, Laura?'

Laura was staring into space.

'Laura,' said Chelsea, poking her arm, 'what do you think?'

Laura blinked. 'About what?'

'Oh for heaven's sake,' said Chelsea, 'you've been in a dream world all evening.'

'A nightmare world, more like,' said Laura with a catch in her voice.

Chelsea appeared not to hear. She had to keep Rob's attention firmly on her. What was it Mum said? 'Sometimes a woman has to take the lead.'

'Come on, Rob,' she said and dragged a still bewildered Rob on to the dance floor.

Jemma tried to look interested in the contents of her glass and wished someone would ask her to dance. Laura sniffed noisily.

'What's wrong?' asked Jemma.

'Oh, just leave me alone,' snapped Laura. 'I'm going to get another drink.'

She blundered across to the Coke bar, blinking furiously in an attempt to stop the tears which threatened to spill over any second.

'Hey, look out!'

Laura felt something wet running down her arm.

'Look where you're going, can't you? That's half my Dr Pepper down the drain.' That voice was familiar. It sounded like Jon.

Laura peered through the semi darkness.

It was Jon.

Laura gulped.

'Hi Jon,' she said. Perhaps there was a God after all.

'Oh, it's you,' he muttered, without quite the degree of enthusiasm Laura would have liked. 'I might have guessed. So you're as clumsy on foot as you are on a bike, I see.'

'Sorry,' said Laura, cursing herself for not appearing more sophisticated. 'I've got a lot on my mind – I wasn't thinking.'

'That,' said Jon, 'is abundantly clear.' Suddenly he brightened. 'Er – have you come here with Sumitha?'

'Not really,' said Laura, who was not about to have her rival intrude on this precious conversation, even if she was now spoken for. 'Did you come with Rob? Chelsea never said.'

'Yes – I think he's hoping that girl Mandy Fincham will be here,' said Jon, with a grin. 'I reckon he's got the hots for her.'

I wonder how that little gem of information will go down with Chelsea, thought Laura.

'Is Sumitha sitting with you?' he persisted.

'No, she's on the floor, dancing,' snapped Laura. And then remembered that *Yell!* magazine said that bitchiness got you nowhere and that snide remarks were a turn off. 'But yes, she is with us,' she admitted grudgingly.

'Oh good,' said Jon. 'Over here, is it?' he added gesturing towards where Jemma sat in splendid isolation.

He headed off in the direction of their table, all the time peering anxiously around the dance floor. Laura thought desperately for something to say. 'Did you have a good summer?' Damn, she thought; that was a naff line for a start.

'What? Oh, yes. Yes, it was as a matter of fact,' said Jon, frowning as he watched Bilu and Sumitha gyrating wildly under the spotlights.

'Did you do loads of drawing?' she asked. *Show an interest in their hobbies*, the article had said.

Jon looked at her properly for the first time.

'Yes I did. How did you know that I draw?'

'Jemma Farrant told me you want to be a cartoonist,' said Laura. 'She's one of my best mates – she lives next door to you.'

'Oh, yes, the chubby one,' Jon said vaguely, his gaze darting round the room.

Sadly, he said that just as they came within earshot of where Jemma was sitting morosely sipping her drink. That's it, thought Jemma, tears pricking behind her eyes. That is it. From now on, I'm giving up calories, carbohydrates and fat. She pushed her Pepsi away – she wasn't sure whether it was a diet one or not and she wasn't taking any chances.

'Is Sumitha related to that guy she's with?' Jon asked. Perhaps there was a perfectly logical explanation for them being together, he thought.

'Very distantly, I think, but not so as it counts,' said Laura. 'Well, put it this way; because he is some sort of distant relative of some cousin a zillion times removed,

63

Sumitha's dad approves of him. Sumitha approves of him because she is madly in love.' Put that in your pipe and smoke it, she thought.

'With Bilu?' said Jon. 'Sumitha fancies Bilu Chakrabarti?' He sounded both incredulous and wounded.

'You know him?' asked Laura.

'Yes – he's in the Sixth Form at my school,' said Jon.

Of course, thought Laura. Sumitha had said he went to Bellborough Court.

'I don't think it is at all a good idea for Sumitha to be seeing him,' continued Jon. 'He's a right self-opinionated, spoiled . . .'

'Well, I'm sure that Sumitha is quite capable of looking after herself,' said Laura. This conversation was not going at all the way she had planned.

'Anyway, he's going around with another girl in the Sixth Form – Natalie someone or other. Mind you, he changes girlfriends like most people change their socks,' he added bitterly.

Just then, Sumitha and Bilu reappeared with Chelsea and Rob.

'Hello, Sumitha, how are you?' said Jon. 'You look great,' he added shyly.

'Hi, Jon,' said Sumitha without taking her adoring eyes off of Bilu's face.

'Well, if it isn't old Joseph,' said Bilu, slapping Jon on the back and causing the contents of his second glass of Dr Pepper to shoot over his shirt. 'Year Eleven night out, is it?

Watching how the big boys perform?' And he laughed loudly at his own wit. Sumitha joined in, although she wasn't exactly sure what she was laughing at.

Jon said nothing. Beside Bilu, he felt clumsy and stupid. Rob shot him a sympathetic glance – he knew Jon was crazy about Sumitha but he got the feeling he was on a loser there. That was the trouble with girls; the ones you just wanted to be good mates with kept coming on strong and the ones you wanted to snog never took a blind bit of notice of you.

They all danced a lot more – all, that is, except Jemma, who by ten o'clock, was feeling really miserable. Everyone seemed to have boys after them except her. She just wanted it to be time to go home.

'This is a cool place, isn't it?' said Sumitha to Bilu.

'Not really my scene,' said Bilu. 'OK for kids, but if you ask me, it's all a bit tame.'

'Well, yes, I suppose it is really,' said Sumitha hurriedly.

He put his arm round Sumitha, who went all weak at the knees. 'I know, let's you and me go burn some rubber,' said Bilu.

Sumitha looked mystified.

'Pardon?' she said.

'The car, silly!' Bilu smirked. 'Let's see how she goes on the open road. We could bomb over to Ditchford Common.'

Sumitha was apprehensive. 'Well,' she said, 'Dad did say just to come here and straight home – and if I don't . . .'

'Oh well, if Daddy's rules mean more to you than an evening with me, then I'll go and find someone who . . .'

'No, no,' interrupted Sumitha in a panic. 'It'll be OK. He'll never find out. They're dumb rules, anyway,' she added boldly, glancing appealingly at her friends who were listening in astonished silence.

'Um, Sumitha,' began Jemma, 'don't you think you ought to . . .'

'Oh loosen up, Jemma – you sound just like your Mummy,' said Sumitha cuttingly. The others exchanged glances. This was all totally out of character. Bilu headed for the door.

'Sumitha, you can't – you'll land yourself right in it with your dad if you don't watch out. Shouldn't you at least phone?' Laura piped in.

Sumitha chewed her lip. Then she took a deep breath and said, 'See you around,' in a voice which didn't sound a bit like her normal one, and ran after Bilu.

Jon let out a long, slow sigh. He stared into his glass for a couple of moments and then, turning to Laura, he said, 'Do you want to dance?'

Laura nodded eagerly. She'd done it. She had driven off the opposition. She had Jon all to herself.

For the next hour, she didn't give her mother's pregnancy or her own approaching sisterhood another thought.

Chapter Twenty-Four

A Night of Surprises

Sumitha sat rigidly in the passenger seat as Bilu took bends at what seemed like breakneck speed. He had put the roof down and the wind was making her eyes water.

'This is some machine, isn't it?' said Bilu, as he accelerated even more. 'It's got ABS, alloy wheels – and just wait till you hear this audio system.' He pressed a button and Mashing Swede filled the air.

He accelerated over a hump back bridge and Sumitha's stomach lurched uncomfortably.

'Can we stop for a bit?' she asked tentatively as the speedometer crept up to eighty.

Bilu turned to look at her. 'Well, yes, if you like,' he said. 'If that's what you want.'

He pulled into a lay-by and switched off the engine.

'And to think I thought you were a timid little thing,' he said, pulling her towards him.

He's going to kiss me, thought Sumitha. Properly. Just wait till I tell the others.

Bilu planted a kiss on her lips and ran his fingers through her hair.

Sumitha closed her eyes. I am in love, she thought. And I like it.

What happened next took Sumitha completely by surprise. Bilu kissed her again, but this time pushing his tongue into her mouth and letting his hands stray into the top of her shirt. He held on to her hair and it hurt. She pulled away hurriedly.

'Hey,' said Bilu. 'What's with you? That's what you wanted to stop for, wasn't it?'

'No – yes – I mean,' began Sumitha. She wasn't going to admit that until that quick kiss in her grandmother's garden in Calcutta she'd never been kissed before – she dreamed about what it would be like but somehow this wasn't quite what she had imagined. In her imaginings, he would gaze into her eyes, and tell her she was exquisitely beautiful and that he would die without her. Then he would kiss her gently on the lips and do some more gazing. She wasn't sure about this fumbling bit.

She gulped. 'I wanted to stop because I didn't like driving so fast,' she admitted.

'Oh yes?' said Bilu mockingly. 'Pull the other one.' He looked at her through half closed eyes. 'You're a funny little thing, aren't you? One minute you are giving me the come on and the next you are acting all prim and proper. But of course, if you don't like being kissed . . .'

'Oh, I do, I do really,' said Sumitha.

'Good,' said Bilu and kissed her again, running his hands up and down her legs.

Sumitha chewed her lip. 'I, er, perhaps we should be getting home,' she stammered. 'You don't want to get into my dad's bad books for being late.'

Bilu threw back his head and roared with laughter.

'Don't you worry about that,' he said. 'I got your dad sussed the first time I met him. For him, I shall be the perfect Bengali boy, all charm, good manners – and celibacy. For you, babe, I aim to be rather different.'

And with that, he turned the ignition, threw the car into gear and with a screech of tyre on tarmac spun the car round and headed back into Leehampton.

What did he mean, giving him the come on? wondered Sumitha as Mashing Swede enquired, *'Tell me girl, can you handle this?'*. Am I really prim and proper? If I am, he won't like me. I'd better change. Fast.

Which was not one of Sumitha's best ideas as events were to show.

Chapter Twenty-Five

Home and Dry?

'They're late, Rajiv.' Mrs Banerji drew back the sitting room curtain and peered out into the street. 'We said eleven-fifteen and it is nearly eleven-thirty. I knew we should have insisted they went with Mrs Gee.'

'Don't worry so, Chitrita,' said her husband, putting down his newspaper. 'We know she is in good hands – I expect there is a lot of traffic.'

Mrs Banerji sighed. Her husband seemed so sure that Bilu was perfection personified; only a few months ago he was forbidding Sumitha to go to clubs at all and now, just because of Bilu, he seemed totally calm about the fact that she was late coming home. And Bilu was driving that flashy car. She didn't approve of young people having everything handed to them on a silver plate but then, the Chakrabartis were very rich. Mrs Banerji knew well enough that, no matter what, he was a seventeen-year-old boy and her daughter was an impressionable and somewhat repressed fifteen-year-old. It didn't take a university education to work out that those were dangerous ingredients.

Just then, the car drew up outside. Mrs Banerji gave up a silent prayer of thanks and sat down in her chair, trying to look nonchalant.

Sumitha and Bilu came in, Sumitha looking somewhat apprehensive, Bilu his normal confident self.

'Mr Banerji, sir, how can I apologise enough?' began Bilu. 'Sumitha felt a little faint – the heat in the club I expect, so I drove very slowly to make sure she was all right. Do please forgive me for being late.'

'That is all right, Bilu,' said Rajiv graciously. 'Don't apologise. And thank you for taking such good care of my daughter.'

Sumitha's eyes nearly popped out of her head. She had expected a lecture for them both.

Her mother kept silent. The high colour on her daughter's cheeks did not quite tally with Bilu's story – and

Mrs Banerji had also noticed the look of guilt that crossed Sumitha's face when illness was mentioned.

'Bed now, I think Sumitha,' said her mother.

'I too shall retire,' said Bilu. 'Thank you so much again for your hospitality, Mrs Banerji – that lamb biryani was so good at supper.' He smiled.

Mind you, he is a nice boy, thought Chitrita. Perhaps I am reading too much into things.

Chapter Twenty-Six

Chelsea's Dad Springs a Surprise

When Chelsea's mum had arrived at the club to fetch the girls, she had been feeling very uptight. Her producer had phoned to say that he didn't want to upset her but he couldn't help feeling that her performance on the show that morning hadn't been up to her sparkling best; Warwick had informed her that he needed eight hundred pounds for the first term's rent at uni, and worst of all, Barry still wasn't home and he hadn't even phoned to say where he was.

Ginny was beginning to feel like those women who kept writing to her agony column – angry with him for being so insensitive and angry with herself for yelling at him so much lately. She knew she hadn't been in the best of moods since the holiday. She did hope nothing had happened to him. Perhaps he was with another woman. Oh no, he couldn't be. He wouldn't. If he was, she'd kill him. Dead.

As they had pulled into Thorburn Crescent, Mrs Gee had uttered an oath under her breath. Completely blocking her driveway was a huge white van, its rear doors wide open and banging in the breeze.

'What the blazes . . . ?' she began. And stopped. Barry was staggering down the drive clutching a pile of copper pans and wearing, of all things, a chef's hat and butcher's apron.

She wound down the window.

'Where on earth have you been?' she snapped, relief that he was all right making her irritable. 'I was worried sick. And whose van is that blocking our drive?'

'Mine,' he said proudly.

'Pardon?' said Chelsea and her mum in unison.

Barry beamed proudly.

'Let me introduce you to the Soup Kitchen. "Soup up your lunch hours with Gee's Ham and Pea." I'm taking it round all the industrial estates and office complexes selling Soup to Go. Good, eh? Come in and I'll tell you all about it.'

Chapter Twenty-Seven
And So to Bed

Late that night, over on Billing Hill, Jon was lying awake wishing he was seventeen and had a fast car. Then Sumitha would want to be with him.

Next door, Jemma was crying into her pillow. She was fat, ugly and no one had danced with her all evening. What's more, Sumitha said she was getting like her mother. She'd have to do something about that. She couldn't end up like Mum. She had to get thin and get a life. She sat up, switched on the light and began drawing up a diet plan.

In Wordsworth Close, Laura was fast asleep, dreaming that Jon was painting her portrait. Except the picture turned out to be of dozens of fat little babies.

And in Thorburn Crescent, Chelsea and Ginny were battling in the kitchen.

'And where are you going to make all this soup then?' shouted Ginny.

'Well, here, initially, and then when I've made enough money, I'll rent a unit,' said Barry calmly.

'Oh great. Oh terrific. So now my kitchen becomes a factory, does it?' shouted Ginny.

'Dad, what about us? What about meals?' said Chelsea. 'What will people think?'

'For God's sake,' shouted Barry, slamming a saucepan lid

down on the counter top and running a hand through his hair, 'I am doing it for *us*. You two apparently need to spend money like water – well, that's what I intend to make. Money. For months, you've been nag, nag, nagging about me getting a job. So, I've got one. Doing the one thing that really interests me. And if for a few months it means putting up with a bit of mess in the kitchen, then it's a small price to pay. Not,' he added sarcastically, 'that either of you ever goes into it voluntarily anyway!'

'But where did the money come from? For the van and all these pots and pans?' asked Ginny.

'A Small Business Enterprise Loan from the bank.'

Ginny sighed. 'More debts, then?'

'Look, the banks are itching to give away cash. I'll pay it off in no time. This is going to be a success. I know it is.'

Ginny tried a smile. 'OK. We'll give it a go. And I'm sorry. You're right. We do need the money and I'm proud you had the idea.'

'Dad, promise me one thing,' said Chelsea.

'What's that?' said Barry.

'Don't take that van anywhere near my school. Ever.'

Now there's an idea, thought Barry. But decided it was best not to comment.

Chapter Twenty-Eight
Meetings and Mayhem

By mid-morning on Sunday, Jemma had enough of watching her mother and brothers making a show of themselves in the leisure pool at the Waterline Golf Country Club.

'Why won't you come in, petal?' called Mrs Farrant from the shallow end, to Jemma's intense embarrassment.

'I'm not swimming,' said Jemma.

Her mother climbed out of the pool and trotted over, water dripping off the frills of her ancient swimsuit.

'But it's lovely,' she began.

'Mum, I said, I am not swimming,' repeated Jemma.

'Oh, sorry, petal,' said her mother, tapping her nose knowingly. 'Not in front of the little ones. I see. Time of the month, is it?'

'Yes, that's it,' lied Jemma.

In fact, Jemma had made a vow to lose two whole stone by Christmas and she was not about to parade about in a swimsuit until she looked slim and sylph-like, like Sumitha. Today she had dressed in black jeans, a black T-shirt and the baggiest sweater she could find – anything to hide her disgustingly bouncy boobs. She felt gross and boring and knew she looked like a globule of solidified fat. But watching her mother and brothers having such a good time made her feel even more fed up, and picking up her book, *Weight Loss Without Worry*, which she had found in the newsagents when she went to collect the Sunday papers, she wandered off outside.

The club house was set in rolling parkland, once the grounds of an old manor house. Mr Farrant, who was already out on the course, had joined partly because he liked the sound of what the advertisers called, *'this superb par 72 course, set among lakes and tumbling streams, affording an ever-changing challenge to the most discerning of golfers,'* but more particularly because when Professor Sir William Kentigan-Fry, leading light of the Pike Research Centre for Hearing Disorders had spoken at the Leehampton General Hospital he had mentioned that he was passionate about golf and a member at the Waterline. Andrew Farrant's great ambition was to move into research and if playing a few rounds with the great Sir K-F would help his cause, then he was not about to pass up the opportunity.

Jemma wandered past the paved veranda, where clusters of chattering women were seated at wooden tables, all looking very suave and slim. She ambled along a path behind the club house till she came to a clump of trees overlooking a small lake.

She settled down to read, pulling off her sweater to use as a pillow and shielding her eyes from the sun with her hand.

She had just got to page six (*FADE AWAY THE FLAB WITH FIBRE AND FIGS – a dieter's best friend is fibre, so eat: bran, baked beans, wholemeal pasta and figs*) when something flew through the branches of the tree and hit her on the shoulder.

'Ouch!' she shrieked, grabbing her right shoulder with her left hand and screwing her eyes up in agony.

'Have I hurt you?' a voice said from behind a tree.

Jemma looked up to see a green blur. Her eyes travelled up a pair of green cord trousers to a cream and green sweater, a worried face and a mop of exceedingly untidy sandy coloured hair.

'I really am awfully sorry,' said the face. Jemma rubbed a hand hastily across her eyes and refocused. A stockily built boy with glasses and a sunburned nose was gazing at her. 'I didn't know there was anyone around here – I was just having a practice swipe, you see. Bit boring waiting for the old man to finish his round.'

He squatted down beside Jemma and surveyed her shoulder anxiously.

'It's OK,' said Jemma. 'I think I'll live. I'm probably not supposed to be over here anyway. I was bored too.'

'Oh, yes, well – er . . .' His gaze left her bruised shoulder and travelled down her T-shirt, lingering halfway.

Jemma grabbed her sweater and pulled it on. He was obviously thinking what a fat slob she was. She clambered to her feet and *Weight Loss Without Worry* fell to the ground. Face up. She stamped her foot on it, grabbed it and stuffed it up her sweater.

'Oh I'm Rupert, by the way – Rupert Kentigan-Fry. Good book?'

'Just revision – really boring,' said Jemma hastily. 'I'm Jemma,' she added, thankful to be anonymous inside her sweater, 'and I think my dad is playing golf with yours – is your father Sir William?' She had never met the son of a Sir before but Rupert seemed quite ordinary, except for the fact that he spoke like something out of a BBC period drama.

'Yes, that's right – so is your father Andrew Farrant? The new chap at the General?'

'Mm,' said Jemma, rubbing her shoulder which was beginning to throb rather badly.

'I say, look, I mean, I ought to do something about your shoulder and all that,' said Rupert. 'What say we go back to the club house and I'll buy you a drink and we can get some plasters or something?'

Jemma giggled. 'I don't think a Band Aid is going to have much effect,' she said. 'It'll be OK, honestly. But a drink would be nice.' At least she had someone to talk to. And someone male to tell her friends about.

Jemma followed him down the pathway and then froze. Heading towards her, arms flapping like a windmill in a hurricane was her mother.

'There you are, petal – I was getting worried,' Mrs Farrant chirruped. 'Daddy's nearly done, and then we can all have some lunch. Oh, er, and who is this?' She looked at Rupert enquiringly, as if expecting him to hand her his credentials.

'This is Rupert,' said Jemma hurriedly. 'Dad's playing with his father.'

'Oh well now, isn't that nice!' gushed Claire. 'I told you

that you would make a friend if you came along, Jemma, didn't I?'

Jemma cringed.

'So you're Sir William's son.'

'Yes, that's right, Mrs Farrant,' said Rupert.

'I said to Jemma, the golf club is just the place for meeting a nice type of . . .'

Jemma interrupted hastily. 'Mum, look – er – I think the twins are annoying that couple over by the barbecue,' she improvised.

'Oh dear, naughty little boys,' muttered Claire and dashed off. Jemma sighed.

'Sorry,' she muttered. 'Mothers. Do you live round here?' asked Jemma as she and Rupert made their way to the bar. Stupid question, she thought. Of course he does or he wouldn't be here.

'Yes, we live at Boughton Court,' he said.

'Boughton Court? That huge stone house with the wrought iron gates?' Jemma gasped.

'Yes, that's the one,' said Rupert in a matter of fact voice. 'Oh look, there's Father and your pa.'

Jemma grinned to herself. She'd never thought of Dad as a pa.

'So you've met Rupert, I see,' said Sir William, smiling and shaking Jemma's hand. 'Did you get in some practice, Rupert – hit a few birdies?'

'Oh, I hit a birdie, yes,' Rupert looked at Jemma, gave her a dig in the ribs and giggled.

Oh yuk, thought Jemma. Why did he have to touch my disgusting bulk?

They walked in silence for a bit.

'You're awfully pretty,' said Rupert suddenly.

Jemma stared at him.

'I was wondering,' said Rupert, 'I mean, could I have your phone number? I'd really like to see you again. Perhaps we could go out somewhere,' he added.

Jemma's heart soared.

'Yes – yes, that would be nice,' she stammered. He might not be David Beckham but he was male. And he seemed to like her. And he did have a very nice smile. And the sunburned nose would clear up soon.

She'd done it. Jemma Farrant had been asked out.

Chapter Twenty-Nine

Laura Lets Rip

While the Farrants and the Kentigan-Frys were making small talk about the excellence of the smoked salmon sandwiches and the awkward sweep to the fourteenth hole, and Jemma was wondering how quickly she could lose another stone, Laura was at home making her feelings known in a somewhat less controlled manner.

'I just want you to know that I think what you have done is positively disgusting!' she shouted as soon as Melvyn set foot inside the front door for Sunday lunch.

'And good morning to you too, Laura!' he said with a twinkle in his eye. 'I take it your mum has told you the good news.'

But Laura had stormed upstairs.

Laura fully intended refusing any lunch, but it turned out to be roast lamb and mint sauce followed by apple charlotte and ice cream and she didn't see why she should starve because of the debauched behaviour of her mother.

'I gave notice on my flat today,' said Melvyn conversationally when Ruth had dished up.

'Good,' said Ruth, nervously eyeing her daughter.

Perhaps, thought Laura hopefully, he was going to do a runner.

'So when shall I start moving my stuff in here?' he continued.

Laura choked on a Brussel sprout.

'You are *not* moving in here?' she exclaimed incredulously.

'Well, of course – after all, your mum is my responsibility now, isn't she?' he said sweetly. 'She needs looking after.'

'But – you can't – I mean, there isn't enough room in this dump for Mum and me, never mind you,' she said, her eyes filling with tears. 'Anyway, we're OK on our own. We don't need anyone else.'

'Well, actually what I thought would be a good idea for us all was . . .' began Melvyn while Ruth bit her fingernails and looked close to tears.

'I don't care what you think,' screamed Laura, slamming down her knife and fork and shooting carrots all over the tablecloth. 'You should have thought before you got my mum into this mess! But then with a pea-sized brain like yours, I don't suppose there is much scope for thinking!'

'Laura!' pleaded Ruth. 'Look love, it'll be . . .'

'HELL!' screamed Laura. 'That's what it will be. And I for one am not stopping around to see it happen. Have your hateful baby, slobber all over your toyboy. See if I care! I'm not stopping here a minute longer!'

She leaped to her feet. More carrots left the plate.

'And where will you go?' enquired Melvyn calmly.

'To my dad!' shouted Laura. 'Because he loves me, even if you two don't! I shall go and live with Dad!'

And so saying, she stormed upstairs to her room.

Mrs Turnbull burst into tears.

Ten minutes later, Laura stalked into the room.

Ruth looked hopeful.

'I've only come,' Laura said dramatically waving a rucksack in the air, 'to say goodbye. I'm leaving. I am going to Dad's. And don't try to stop me.'

'OK,' said Melvyn.

Ruth shot him a glance. 'Look, why don't we . . .'

But Laura had gone.

Chapter Thirty
Ginny Lets It Slip

'What's for lunch?' asked Chelsea.

'You can choose,' said her father. 'Try my Carrot and Orange soup, or my Bouillabaisse, or there's some rather nice Leek and Potato.'

'What? Soup? Is that all? We usually have a roast,' she said.

'Oh, there's cold ham and cheese as well,' said her father. 'And a lemon soufflé for afterwards. But I need to try out these soups before I hit the road with them tomorrow.'

'God, it's so humiliating. My father a street vendor,' cried Chelsea and stormed out of the kitchen. Straight into her mother. 'Can't you stop him?' demanded Chelsea.

'I'm not sure that putting my oar in will do much good,' said her mother.

'You have been fighting a lot lately, anyway,' said Chelsea.

'Not fighting,' corrected Ginny, 'just having a few differences of opinion.'

'Pretty noisy ones,' commented Chelsea. 'What about?'

'Oh, well . . .' Ginny sighed. 'Money and jobs and then I said I envied Ruth having the baby and . . .' Ginny stopped and bit her tongue.

'Mrs Turnbull? She's having a baby? Oh wow,' said Chelsea. 'Cute.'

'Yes, well, I'm sworn to secrecy so for heaven's sake don't let on I told you. Come to think of it, you could help there.'

'What, baby-sit and stuff? But Laura'll do that,' said Chelsea.

'No, not that. It's just that I get the feeling that Laura is not all that impressed with her mum being pregnant,' said Ginny. 'In fact, she's pretty cut up about it.'

'So that's why she was in such a mood last night,' said Chelsea as light dawned. 'So Mrs T's going to marry the geek – I mean, Melvyn, is she?'

'Well, I don't know,' admitted Ginny. 'But I do know he's going to be moving in and I don't think . . .'

'Laura will go spare!' said Chelsea.

'Perhaps you can make her see it's not all bad. Help make Ruth's life easier. But you won't say a word till Laura tells you herself, will you?'

'OK,' said Chelsea. 'Hey, why did you say you envied Mrs T?'

'Oh, nothing,' said her mother. 'Put the salt and pepper out, will you?' And she made a hasty retreat.

Chapter Thirty-One

A Slight Change of Plan

Laura's dad and the Bestial Betsy were enjoying a rare treat – Sunday lunch on their own. Sonia and Daryl were spending the weekend with their grandmother so they'd opened a bottle of sparkling wine to celebrate exchanging contracts on their new house and were discussing the merits of distressed pine kitchen units over marble topped butchers' tables.

'It's nice to have a bit of peace, isn't it?' said Peter. 'Oh, I love the kids dearly,' he added hastily, seeing a frown appear on Betsy's face, 'but still, we deserve a bit of time to ourselves.'

Betsy nodded and moved round to sit on his lap. 'I was thinking,' she said, 'now we've got the new house and everything, why don't we get ma–'

Just then the doorbell shrilled. And whoever was outside was not about to take their finger off.

'Who on earth can that be?' said Peter. 'All right, all right, keep your hair on, I'm coming.'

Betsy sighed. Just as she had got him in the right mood too. It seemed the Fates were against her.

Peter went to the door, a trifle unsteadily on account of the three glasses of wine.

Standing there looking forlorn was his daughter.

'Can I come in?' she said.

Oh brilliant, thought Betsy. One day to ourselves and she turns up.

'Can we talk alone?' said Laura, nodding in Betsy's direction.

'I'll make some coffee,' said Betsy with a sigh, and retreated into the kitchen.

'I'll have the proper stuff,' called Peter. Betsy was currently into herbal teas and dandelion coffees, all of which tasted to Peter like a mixture of bath salts and seaweed. 'How on earth did you get here?' he said, turning to his daughter.

'I cycled,' said Laura. 'It's an emergency. You'll have to do something.'

'But what is it? What have I to do something about?' asked Mr Turnbull.

'It's Mum,' said Laura, her eyes filling with tears.

'Mum? Why? What's happened? Is she ill?' said Peter.

Ah-ha, thought Laura. So you do still care.

What's going on? thought Betsy who had pressed her ear up to the serving hatch in order not to miss anything.

'It's worse than that,' she said dramatically. 'She's . . .'

But before she could finish, the telephone shrilled. Peter jumped up to answer it.

'Hello? . . . oh, hi there Ruth,' said Peter.

First the daughter, then the poxy ex-wife, thought Betsy irritably, spooning coffee into the cafetière.

'Pardon? You're what?' Peter sounded astonished.

'Well, well. Are you pleased? Well then, that's

wonderful – congratulations! Well, yes, actually, she's just arrived. Oh dear. She is? OK, then, thanks for letting me know. No, no, don't worry, I'll see to it.'

'That was Mum,' he said, sitting down at the table. 'She phoned to tell me the news.'

'Oh, so she finally got round to telling you, did she?' said Laura viciously. She was a bit annoyed that she hadn't had time to be the bearer of ill tidings. 'God, Dad, you must feel sick to your stomach – I know I do.'

Peter laughed. 'No Laura, it's the expectant mum that feels that way. And in any case, I think it's great news. I'm very happy for her. Aren't you?'

'No, I am not!' snapped Laura. 'How can I be happy when soon the entire world will know that my mother is having an illegitimate kid by some idiot she met a few months ago? The whole thing's obscene. It's humiliating. That's why I'm moving in with you.'

Peter gulped. 'Pardon?'

'I'm moving in here – I've brought some clothes. You can fetch the rest of my stuff in the car later.'

'Well now, look love,' Peter stammered, 'I don't honestly think that . . .'

At which point the door opened and in came Betsy, bearing a tray and with two points of very high colour on her cheeks.

'What's going on?' she asked in a tight voice.

'That was Ruth on the phone, love,' began Peter. 'She's going to have a baby.'

'That's nice,' said Betsy grimly.

'And Laura is not very happy about it,' said Peter lamely.

'So I'm coming to live here,' said Laura.

'Not a good idea really,' said Betsy, dumping the tray on the table. 'I do recall you once saying that you would never cross the threshold for as long as I was with your father. So actually living here would be terribly tedious for you.'

'Yes, but that was . . .' began Laura.

'Oh, I know that was then when it suited you to make our relationship the subject of your latest fit of dramatics,' said Betsy, ignoring the warning glances that Laura's dad was hurling at her. 'And of course, this is now, when your nose is out of joint because of the baby. But really, we couldn't let you take a decision that goes against all your moral principles, now could we?'

'You can't speak to me like that,' stammered Laura. 'Dad – say something. Tell her to mind her own business.'

'Well, now love,' began Peter who really only wanted a quiet life, 'I don't honestly think that it is a very good idea. I mean, when we've moved you can come over and see us and . . .'

'Oh great. Terrific. Bloody wonderful,' cried Laura, jumping up and sending a mug of coffee flying. 'This is all your doing, you big-nosed cow,' she said, jabbing a finger in Betsy's direction. 'You've turned my own father against me.'

'Laura, Laura, calm down,' said Peter. 'I'm not turning against you. I am just wondering whether you living here would be sensible. I mean, what about school? What about your friends? The new house is eight miles from Leehampton. And what about Mum – she needs you, she loves you.'

'Oh yes,' snapped Laura through her tears. 'If she loves me so much, why is she having another baby? I suppose she's got bored with me and wants a replacement model. Besides, she's got that jerk to keep her happy.'

'Love,' said Betsy sipping her dandelion coffee, 'doesn't come rationed. Just because your mum has a new man in her life and is having another baby doesn't mean that her love for you will diminish any. But if you walked out now, she would be devastated, and you would probably end up not loving yourself much.'

'And who do you think you are to preach to me?' cried Laura. 'You stole my dad, now you're trying to tell me what to do. Well, back off, you . . . you tart!'

'Laura!' shouted Peter. 'Apologise to Betsy!'

'Why should I? Come to think of it, it's all her fault anyway. If she hadn't seduced you away from Mum, Melvyn wouldn't have turned up and Mum wouldn't be pregnant.'

'I am waiting for an apology,' said her father through clenched teeth.

'Well, you've got a blimmin' long wait then,' said Laura. She flounced into the hall, picked up her rucksack and stormed out, slamming the front door behind her.

Peter sank into a chair.

'So much for a day of rest,' he said, rubbing his eyes. 'Still, at least I am getting practice for when your Sonia gets to that age.'

'Sonia,' said Betsy, 'has been properly brought up. Sonia won't behave like that.'

I wouldn't count on it, thought Peter. I wouldn't count on it at all.

Chapter Thirty-Two

Art for Art's Sake?

Laura cycled furiously out of the village on to the Leehampton Road, tears blurring her vision and causing her to wobble precariously. She was determined not to go home, well not yet anyway. Let them all worry about her, let them realise what they were doing to her.

The trouble was, where should she go? Then she had a bright idea. She'd call in on Jemma – she was always sympathetic. And she'd tell Jemma about the baby and see what reaction she got.

But there was no one in at 49 Billing Hill. She rang the bell several times, and even peered through the front window. Nothing. Now even her friends were deserting her in her hour of need.

'You won't get an answer, they've gone out for the day.' Jon was leaning over the hedge, grinning at her, his hands covered in cycle grease.

'Oh, hi,' she said as her heart did a double back somersault and pike into her mouth. Oh, no, my face, she thought. I know I look all red-eyed and puffy; why do I always look so awful when Jon's around?

'I wanted Jemma,' she mumbled, trying to keep her face averted. But I'd rather have you, she added silently.

'I guessed,' said Jon, flicking hair out of his eyes with his wrist and succeeding in smudging oil on his cheeks. 'Any message?'

Yes, I think you are the most gorgeous guy in the world.

'No, no it's OK, thanks,' she said.

'See you, then,' Jon turned to go back into the house.

On the other hand, thought Laura.

'I was going to ask your advice,' she called.

Jon turned, looking puzzled.

'Well, I've got to do all the publicity stuff for our school musical. You know, posters and programmes and things. We're doing . . .'

'*Oliver!* I know, lucky things,' said Jon. 'I can't wait to get to Lee Hill, then I can get involved in designing stage drops and things. Bellborough's a bit thin on the theatricals.'

'Well, what I was going to say was,' said Laura. 'I mean, would you mind having a look at my ideas and seeing

91

whether you think they'd work. I mean, being brilliant at art and stuff, you'd know.'

'Yes, OK then,' said Jon, trying not to look too pleased at being asked. 'Do you want to come in now and show me what you've got? Mum and Dad are both out, so we've got the place to ourselves.'

Cool. She got to spend an hour or so with Jon and everyone else could worry themselves sick about her. Serve them all right.

Jon's bedroom was amazing. You couldn't see one scrap of wall because of all the posters and pictures and cartoons pinned to huge cork pinboards all round the room. There were portraits of cats and dogs, caricatures of politicians, the royal family, film stars – even one of her favourite band, Bag Handlers. And dominating the wall over his bed was a pastel sketch of a young girl. The subject was unmistakable. It was Sumitha.

Jon caught Laura eyeing it.

'I'm not sure I've caught her expression quite right,' he mused, 'I had to do it all from memory. I don't suppose you've got a photograph of her, have you – I mean, a group school photo or anything?'

'No I haven't,' said Laura shortly. 'But you could always ask Bilu,' she added maliciously.

Jon glowered.

Laura relented. 'Now about these posters . . .'

'Oh yes, right,' said Jon. 'I'll just grab some paper.'

He stretched over to his bedside table and picked up a sheaf of paper and dumped it on the bed. On top was the sketch he'd done at summer school.

'That's me!' said Laura in surprise.

'Oh, yes, well – just doodling,' he said hastily, shoving it to the bottom of the pile. How embarrassing! He hadn't even realised he had kept the thing.

He drew me, thought Laura. And he had it by his bed.

'When did you do that?' said Laura.

'Oh, ages ago,' said Jon. 'I don't even remember doing it.'

So it came from your deep subconscious, thought Laura, who had read her *Psychology Part One* from cover to cover. I am the object of your affections but you are not ready to acknowledge that, she thought silently. I can wait.

'The hair is amazing, isn't it?' said Jon.

'What, this ginger mess?' said Laura in surprise. 'I loathe it.'

'Not *your* hair, silly – Sumitha's,' he said. 'Black hair is so – so striking. But very difficult to get right in a portrait. Anyway, let's get on – what sort of ideas had you got for the posters?'

The rest of the afternoon passed quickly. Laura, who was brilliant with words, had some great ideas for poster catchphrases – *Do you want some more? Come and see Lee Hill School's production of* Oliver! – *and consider yourself one of us!* – and Jon sketched out some great designs for programme covers and flysheets.

At five o'clock, Laura was assailed once more by hunger pangs and decided to go home after all.

'Come over when you've done the drafts and we'll take a look,' said Jon.

'See you soon,' said Laura and cycled off.

As Jon was about to close the front door an unfamiliar car pulled up outside. To his surprise, his mother was sitting in the passenger seat, talking animatedly to a guy he didn't recognise. Then to his amazement, she leaned across and kissed the driver on the cheek.

'Who was that guy?' said Jon casually as his mother switched the kettle on.

'Oh,' said Anona. 'Er, that's just a guy from my design course. He gave me a lift home – my wretched car's got a flat battery. Make the tea, there's a dear. I'm just going to nip upstairs for a shower.'

By the time Jon had made the tea, emptied the pot, started again because he forgot to put the tea bags in, and eaten three Penguin biscuits, his mother finished her shower, and his father was back from golf.

'Good game, Dad?' asked Jon.

'Huh,' said his father.

'What's wrong, Henry?' asked Mrs Joseph, pouring tea.

'Think I'm losing my touch – 15 over par – disgusting!' he said. 'I may be unfit, but I used to have a damn good swing and a keen eye for a ball.'

'Old age, that's what it is, Dad!' said Jon teasingly.

At which his father threw him a cutting glance and

stomped off upstairs. It was only then that Jon realised that his mum hadn't given Dad the usual welcome home kiss. And that his dad didn't seem even to have noticed.

Chapter Thirty-Three

Jemma Tells All

Jemma spent the whole of Monday telling everyone about Rupert.

'What's he like?' asked Chelsea during lunch break.

'He was really friendly and nice,' said Jemma.

'But is he buff?' demanded Sumitha. 'Bilu is *so* buff.'

'Mmmm,' said Jemma non-commitally. She had to admit that hunk was not really the first word to spring to mind when contemplating Rupert.

'And he's got a lovely smile,' she added. That bit was true, at least.

'Bilu's got the most amazing smile,' said Sumitha. Laura raised her eyes heavenwards and Chelsea pulled a face behind Sumitha's back. They were all getting a little tired of hearing about the marvel that was Bilu.

'Has Bilu got loads of girlfriends, being so gorgeous and all?' asked Laura craftily. After all, Jon had hinted that monogamy was not high on Bilu's list of priorities.

'No, of course not!' snapped Sumitha. 'He told me I am the only one for him.'

Oh yes, thought Laura.

'When do we get to meet this Rupert?' asked Chelsea.

'Soon,' promised Jemma. When I'm thin and his nose has stopped peeling.

Chapter Thirty-Four

Things Get Complicated

During the next few weeks, everyone was absorbed with concerns of their own.

Laura, who was getting a bit tired of Jemma and Sumitha hogging the limelight with rundowns on their love lives, decided to break the news about the baby one lunch hour. She was amazed to find that everyone thought she was really lucky.

'Oh, that's brilliant,' said Chelsea, trying to look suitably surprised even though she knew already. 'Cute. Dinky. Oh, can I get to hold it when it's born?'

'You can take it on a one-way ticket to nowhere for all I care,' said Laura.

'I don't know why you're fed up,' said Sumitha. 'Think of all the baby-sitting cash you can earn. I was too young to look after Sandeep when he was born – you've got it made.'

That's a point, thought Laura.

'You'll get all the best bits,' said Jemma. 'The twins were really adorable when they were tiny but now I have no privacy, get my eyeliner used as crayons and have to sit through eighteen re-runs of *Tellytubbies*. By the time this baby gets to be the twins' age, you'll be away at uni. Do you want it to be a boy or a girl?'

But the moment when Laura accepted her impending sisterhood as something to be endured, if not positively welcomed, came one wet Saturday morning when Jon was at her house showing Laura how to draw silhouettes for the programme covers. They were sitting at the kitchen table, surrounded by paper, pens and pastels when Laura's mum arrived back from the shops.

'Look what I found for the baby,' she said holding up a minute lemon sleeping suit with a penguin on the front. 'Isn't it sweet?'

Laura glared.

Oh whoops, I've put my foot in it again, thought Mrs Turnbull as she made a hasty retreat.

'You didn't tell me your mum was having a baby,' said Jon accusingly. 'That's great.'

'I'm glad you think so,' said Laura. 'It's bad enough having a mother who goes around with someone half her age, all luvvy duvvy and holding hands. But a baby? Give me strength.'

'Think yourself lucky, Laura,' he said. 'At least your mum and . . . er . . .'

'Melvyn,' groaned Laura.

'Melvyn, are happy. My parents seem to be like strangers living in the same house right now.'

Laura wasn't sure what to say.

'My mum and dad were like that before they got divorced,' she said.

Oh no, that's not what I meant it to come out like, she thought, cringing.

'Well, um, maybe they are both working too hard,' she suggested hurriedly, seeing the miserable look on Jon's face. 'Your mum is doing a course, isn't she?'

Jon nodded glumly.

'Well, I expect it's that then – doing that all day, and getting to meet new people and everything. It's bound to be tiring.' She hoped she sounded both comforting and mature.

It's the meeting new people bit that bothers me, thought Jon. But decided to change the subject.

'Babies are notoriously difficult to draw,' he said thoughtfully – 'I don't suppose your mum would let me try sketching it when it arrives, would she? I mean, if she didn't mind. It would be a real bonus for my portfolio.'

Mind? I won't give her the chance to mind, thought Laura, if it means Jon coming round more often. Perhaps this baby will have its uses yet.

Chapter Thirty-Five

Moving News

Laura's mum had stopped throwing up and started worrying about how to fit a baby into their already overcrowded two bedroom semi.

'We'll move,' said Melvyn, calm as ever.

'But we can't afford it,' protested Ruth. 'Can we?' she added hopefully.

'Look,' he said, 'I've got a bit put by and with what you would get for this house, we could afford a deposit on something bigger. We need at least three bedrooms, and I reckon four would be good – then I could have one for my computer stuff and there'd still be one for Laura and one for the baby.'

Ruth looked excited. 'I could pick up some details from the estate agent on my way to the ante-natal clinic tomorrow,' she said. 'Laura will be over the moon.'

Chapter Thirty-Six

Diet Decoys

As the weeks passed, Jemma dieted more and more intensely but her regime was not without its problems. She wore baggy sweaters to hide what she thought was an obscene amount of flesh, and even went to the expense of buying a school sweater two sizes bigger than her usual one. Breakfast was no problem because her mum was too tied up with the twins and Sammy to see what she ate. On the way to school, she would ditch the peanut butter sandwiches, chocolate biscuits and slices of quiche that her mother insisted on packing for her into the rubbish bin at the bus stop and substitute them with a couple of carrots and an apple pinched from the larder before she left. Supper was a little more tricky. Her mother kept exhorting her to eat up because she needed all her strength, but she had devised a method whereby she ate all the vegetables first, and then kicked Daniel or Luke under the table till they yelled. Then, while her mother was doing the 'Who's a poor little lambkin, then?' routine she removed every fattening item into a plastic bag.

Occasionally, her mother on seeing an empty plate would tell her not to eat so fast, and Jemma would smile sweetly and say, 'But it's so delicious,' and Mrs Farrant would ruffle her hair and say, 'Thank you petal,' and the crisis would pass.

The trouble was, there was a limit to how often she could kick Daniel. Some nights she had to eat at least four mouthfuls of fattening stuff and that really bothered her. Every morning she weighed herself, even though the diet books said you should only do it once a week; and every night she measured her thighs, her upper arms, her waist – and her detestable boobs.

What was more, Rupert had telephoned the week after the golf club do and invited her out to the cinema. Then he had phoned a couple of days later to cancel because he said he was ill. She was perfectly sure he wasn't – it was just that he couldn't bring himself to take a fat slob out. The worst part was that having told her friends about this great guy who chatted her up and asked her out, she was now going to have to admit to being dumped before she'd even started. Maybe she shouldn't say anything for a while.

Chapter Thirty-Seven

From Good

Laura was counting the days until half-term. She had acquired a bottle of Raven Raver hair dye from the chemist and intended transforming herself into a thing of beauty. All her visits to Jon's house – and there had been plenty, because she made sure she never got things *quite* right – had been purely platonic. She had waited in vain for him to profess his undying love, clasp her to his manly chest and smother her with kisses. But he kept going on about Sumitha's gorgeous black eyes and her wonderful black hair. Well, Laura couldn't do much about her eyes but the hair was a different matter. All her hopes were now pinned on the Raven Raver.

For Sumitha, the past few weeks had been the best ever. On two occasions, Bilu had come to stay and taken her out to the most amazing places. Last week they drove thirty miles to Wellingford and went to a night club called The Purple Pig (although they had told her dad they were going to the cinema to see the latest Bollywood extravaganza). Sumitha had had a drink called Nights of Passion that made her head go all fluffy and her legs tingle. When they got in the car to go home, Bilu had leaned across and kissed her and said 'You're learning – we'll make a little raver of you yet' which made her feel really sophisticated. Then she fell asleep and Bilu had to shake her awake outside her house.

Chapter Thirty-Eight

... To Bad

Things weren't going so well for Chelsea. She had made the grave error of agreeing to go shopping with her mum on Saturday and it was an unmitigated disaster.

They were in Hot Threadz, and Chelsea was browsing through the boleros, when she saw her mother sauntering out of the changing rooms in a pair of capris and a T-shirt which said 'Little Miss Wonderful' on it.

'Mum!' Chelsea grabbed her arm. 'You're not going to buy those, are you?'

'Why not?' said her mum, twirling in front of the mirror and causing her cellulite to go into overdrive. 'I've been really miserable lately. Thought I was losing my verve. Silly, isn't it? So I thought I'd cheer myself up – Dad says we've got to cut back on spending, but this lot is cheap.'

'Very,' said Chelsea wryly. 'Mum, you are too old for stuff like that.'

'Nonsense!' said her mother brightly, 'you're as old as you feel. And besides, it's no good going through life all bland and colourless. I feel like making a statement.'

'Mum, the only statement you're making is that your legs are too big for capris,' said Chelsea. 'Get some track-suit trousers.'

'Kids!' chirruped Ginny to the assistant who was watching the charade in some amazement. 'No sense of flair!'

Mothers! thought Chelsea, walking out of the shop while her mother, unabashed, purchased the ghastly gear. They should carry a government health warning. Then she saw something that stopped her dead in her tracks. Across the concourse, outside See Dees music shop, was Bilu Chakrabarti. And a girl. In an embrace. A very tight embrace. Oh knickers, thought Chelsea. What do I tell Sumitha?

Chapter Thirty-Nine

I Hate Her

Chelsea's mortification didn't stop with her mother. Her dad had been to London to record the *Superchef* programme and her mother had done a piece about it in the *Echo*.

LOCAL MAN COOKS UP A STORM!
Barry Gee, husband of our very own columnist, Ginny Gee, last week took part in the first round of ITV's popular Superchef *contest. Barry (50), a catering consultant from Leehampton, prepared a selection of what he calls 'country cooking from the regions' and . . .*

'Catering consultant?' queried Chelsea.

'Well, I wasn't going to have them say he drove a van round town,' muttered her mother.

'But Dad, did you win?' asked Chelsea. She certainly wasn't having her friends watch if he made a complete prat of himself.

'Watch and see,' he said, his expression giving nothing away. 'Anyway, we are not allowed to disclose the results until after transmission.'

As if all this were not enough, Mandy Fincham was really getting up Chelsea's nose. At last week's rehearsal, Mr Horage had said, 'You make an excellent Nancy, Mandy,' and Chelsea had muttered under her breath, 'That's because playing a slut comes naturally.' Only Miss McConnell had been standing right behind her and heard, and sent her to the Head who gave her a detention and a diatribe on the evils of malicious gossip and slanderous talk. What was even worse was that Rob thought the sun shone out of Mandy's – well, left ear.

The real crunch came a few days later. Chelsea, who had been collecting the papier mâché bowls which the art department had made for the workhouse dining room scene, wandered into the school hall to find Sumitha after the rehearsal had finished. There was no sign of her friend but, partly concealed by the curtains, she caught sight of Rob. And Mandy Fincham. Kissing.

So great was the shock that she fell over a chair, dropped the pile of bowls and at the clatter Rob and Mandy sprang guiltily apart.

'Oh, it's OK, it's only Chelsea,' said Mandy, draping her arm over Rob's shoulder. 'I thought it was the Horrific Horage.'

'Rob . . . what are you doing?' stammered Chelsea.

'Oh, er, well, we were just rehearsing the kissing scene bit,' he said dropping his eyes and turning a bright shade of cerise.

'Well it didn't look much like a rehearsal to me!' shouted Chelsea. 'But then, if you want to consort with a slag, you go right ahead. Don't mind me!'

Mandy laughed, a high pitched brittle laugh. 'We won't, don't worry!' she sneered. 'Why should we?'

Chelsea ran out of the hall, straight into Laura.

'I hate her! I hate her! I hate her!' she cried and burst into tears.

'I think,' said Laura, 'we should go to a coffee shop on the way home.'

After two hot chocolates and a large blueberry muffin, Chelsea felt marginally better.

'If you really want Rob that much,' said Laura, 'you'll have to make him see that you're much better than Mandy. Win him over with your charm.'

Which is just what my mother would say, thought Chelsea.

'God, boys are so fickle!' she said. 'How could he?'

'Well, look,' said Laura, reasonably. 'You can't really call him fickle. I mean, you're not exactly boyfriend and girlfriend, are you? If you were going out properly, then you'd have every right to have a showdown.'

'Which reminds me,' said Chelsea, and told Laura about seeing Bilu with an unknown girl.

'So do I tell Sumitha or not?' she asked.

'Better not – not yet, anyway,' Laura said. 'She'd be so upset and besides, perhaps he was breaking up with this girl because he'd met Sumitha and it was just a farewell kiss.'

'Some farewell,' said Chelsea.

Chapter Forty

Jon Steps In

Jon was getting seriously worried. The week before, while he was cycling to the library, he had seen his mother and that man going into Finch's Antique Gallery, laughing and giggling like a couple of kids. And yesterday, his mum had been late home from college again.

'Where have you been?' his father asked grumpily.

'Oh, it was Vernon's birthday, so a group of us went to Liam's Tavern for a quick one on the way home.'

'Oh,' said Henry, meekly. 'Meet anyone interesting, did you? Potential clients?' Jon wanted to shake him. Can't you see what is happening, Dad? he said silently. Do something. Now. Before it's too late.

There was nothing for it – he would have to get his father on his own, to have a heart to heart with him before it was too late. And he thought he had an idea that Dad would not be able to resist.

'Dad,' he said that morning, 'I don't suppose you'd take me round a golf course one day. Just for a practice.'

Henry positively beamed. 'Of course, of course, if you'd enjoy it – I didn't think you were interested.'

'Well, I'd like to see just what it is that fires you up, Dad,' lied Jon.

'Terrific, super – we'll go next week.' And for the first time in a long while, Henry looked exceedingly happy.

Chapter Forty-One

The Mums Have a Heart-to-Heart

It had been weeks since the mums had met up for a chat and Claire Farrant missed it. There seemed so little to occupy her these days with the twins at nursery and Sam at school.

Still, it would be half-term in a couple of days, which

would mean all the little ones would be home. I'd better start baking cakes and making Jemma's favourite lasagne, bread and butter pudding and those sticky caramel flapjacks, she thought. She's been off her food lately and needs tempting with lots of nice goodies.

It was while she was in the supermarket stocking up with ingredients that she bumped into Ruth and Ginny. Ruth was in a mild state of shock, having just surveyed the cost of baby buggies, nappies and towelling sleepsuits, and was compensating by buying copious quantities of chocolate spread, bananas and red cabbage to assuage her latest cravings, and Ginny was looking for 'Two for the Price of One' offers on blusher and nail polish in pursuit of her new economy drive.

'Why don't you come back and have lunch with me?' suggested Claire, and neither of them missed the faint note of pleading in her voice. 'It's been so long.'

'I'd love to, but I said I'd call in on Chitrita,' said Ginny. 'She sounded a bit down. And then I've got two features to research.'

'We'll ring her and invite her round too. It won't take long. There's some white wine in the fridge,' she added.

'You're on!' said Ginny.

Since only Ginny had seen Ruth since she discovered she was pregnant, the first ten minutes of lunch were taken up with congratulations, and a 'Rather you than me' from Jon's mum, who had popped in to borrow some of the twins' tracing paper and decided to abandon making an

Art Deco lampshade and eat lunch instead, and a 'Oh, I do envy you' from Jemma's mum.

'And is Laura thrilled?' asked Claire, tossing Thousand Island dressing into the salad bowl.

'Not so as you would notice,' said Ruth wryly. 'Apparently I have brought shame and ignominy upon our house. Melvyn, on the other hand, is another story – you'd think he was the first male in the history of evolution to father a child. He goes around with a permanent grin on his face.' She grimaced.

'Although I guess that will be wiped off his face when he realises how much we'll have to spend on a cot and buggy and nappies and . . .'

'Oh, don't worry about all that,' said Claire airily. 'I can lend you loads of stuff – we had to double up when I had the twins, you see. Oh, but they are so lovely when they are tiny, aren't they?' she added, going all dreamy.

'Chelsea tells me Sumitha has a boyfriend,' said Ginny, turning to Chitrita. 'I thought,' she added sweetly, 'that Rajiv would not permit friendships with the opposite sex.'

Mrs Banerji sighed.

'Rajiv seems to think that Bilu is the ideal boy. Oh, he is distantly related to some aunt or cousin of Rajiv's and that is supposed to be recommendation enough. Me, I am not so sure. I feel uneasy about the whole thing.'

The others waited expectantly.

'The other day, they went out supposedly to the cinema to see that new sci-fi film they are all on about – but when

110

they returned, Sumitha was obviously suffering from the effects of drink,' sighed Chitrita.

'No!' they chorused.

'I am sure of it,' said Chitrita. 'She said it was travel sickness but that child has never been car sick in her life. And besides, her breath smelled most strange.'

'Did you ask her?' asked Ginny.

Chitrita shook her head. 'No,' she admitted. 'Bilu sounded so convincing and – well, he was a guest.'

'And as such should not be putting your daughter at risk,' insisted Ginny sternly. 'And Sumitha?'

'Well, when I asked Sumitha about the film – you know, the plot, what happened and so forth – she was very vague and changed the subject as fast as she could. And she looked very guilty.'

'Well, I think you should make your feelings known, Chitrita,' said Ginny. 'Tell Bilu and Sumitha what you will and won't allow and make sure they stick to it. Before it's too late.'

It was a remark Mrs Banerji was going to wish she had heeded sooner.

'Claire,' she said turning to Mrs Farrant, 'I have a favour to ask you. Ellie has to go into hospital for an operation – it wasn't a bug, apparently, but gallstones or some such thing. Anyway, would you take over the running of the crèche? Just for a few months? Please.'

Everyone waited for the excuses about not being able to leave the house, or the little ones.

'I'd love to,' she said. 'To be honest, it'll be great to get out of the house and Andrew will be delighted. He believes in women having outside interests.'

'I wish Henry did,' said Mrs Joseph, nibbling on a stick of celery. 'Ever since I started my course, he's been like a bear with a sore head. Doesn't like his routine upset or his meals five minutes later than usual. And now that he's talking about taking up jogging . . .'

'Henry – jogging?' said Ginny, trying not to laugh at the thought of the florid features and ample abdomen of Henry Joseph bouncing around the pavements of Billing Hill.

Anona nodded. 'I was saying to Vernon only the other day . . .'

'Who's Vernon?' they all asked, interest immediately awakened.

'Oh, just a guy on my course,' said Anona dismissively.

Oh yes, thought the others.

'Anyway, I was telling him about Henry's mood swings and new obsession with fitness and he reckons it's a mid-life crisis. I mean. Henry's had high blood pressure for ages; he takes pills for it and everything. But he's never been one to worry about keeping fit and trim. But now, I find him reading Jon's rugby training manual and trying out some of the exercises. He was purple from the effort.'

'Men do funny things at this age,' said Ginny dryly.

'Talking of work, has Barry had any luck yet?' asked Mrs Farrant.

Ginny shrugged. 'Haven't you heard? He has bought a

van which he drives round town selling soup in poly-styrene cartons. And don't you dare laugh!'

'Sounds like a good idea,' said Mrs Banerji. 'Those industrial estates are miles from the shops and who wants to live on sandwiches all day?'

'I suppose so,' said Ginny. She took another sip of wine. 'Chelsea doesn't think much of it.'

'When did kids ever think much of what their parents try to do?' said Mrs Banerji. 'At least this *Oliver!* thing seems to be occupying them pretty well.'

Ruth nodded. 'We haven't had a crisis or a tantrum for four whole days. This half-term could turn out to be the most peaceful yet.'

Which when you consider it, was a rather reckless thing to say.

Chapter Forty-Two

Half-term High

It had been Sandeep's birthday on Saturday and the Banerjis had taken him out for a pizza with some of his schoolmates in the evening.

Driving home from the restaurant, Sandeep poked Sumitha in the ribs.

'Look,' he said.

'Oh, what is it, pain?' muttered Sumitha, who after three hours in the company of seven juveniles had had enough.

Sandeep pointed.

On the pavement, outside the Contrary Cockerel, was Bilu. With his arms round a girl. Sumitha gasped.

There had to be an explanation. *She* was Bilu's girl-friend. He'd said so.

Mrs Banerji had seen Bilu too. She was about to make a comment but thought better of it. She would just have to keep an even more careful eye on things than before. Bilu, it seemed, was not quite as pure as everyone seemed to believe.

Chapter Forty-Three

Jemma Gets a Date

On Monday, Jemma received the long awaited call from Rupert, who it seemed, had been ill after all – with glandular fever.

'I've still got a few days before I'm allowed back to school,' he said, 'and I thought, well, I mean, would you like to go and see the new Spielberg film?'

'Yes, that would be great,' said Jemma, tucking the telephone under her chin and hugging her knees with excitement. 'When?'

'Tonight?' said Rupert. 'Father's got to go to some Masonic do in Leehampton so he'll pick you up and drop us off at the cinema.'

'Great,' said Jemma. It had happened. She'd been invited out by a boy.

Jemma spent three hours emptying the contents of her wardrobe on to the floor and bemoaning the fact that she had nothing to wear. In the end she settled for a pair of black trousers and a pink T-shirt. It was the first time she had dared to go out without a baggy sweater down to her knees but she had lost nearly a stone in weight and thought she might just risk it.

'Only another stone to go,' she told herself, 'and I'll be bearable.'

Her mother, meanwhile, was intent on giving Jemma a little pep talk.

'Now Jemma, you haven't been out with a boy before,' she began. 'Not that Rupert of course would ever put a foot wrong – such a nice family – but even so, you must remember that you are a girl and he is a boy.'

'You don't say, Mum,' said Jemma. 'You amaze me.'

'Don't be rude, dear,' said her mother. 'Just treat him like a friend – after all, you are too young for boyfriends. And with Sir William picking you up and bringing you back, I suppose everything will be all right.'

'Mum, we are going to see a film, not take part in an orgy,' said Jemma. Her mother glared at her and went off to vacuum the entire house, repot the hanging basket in the front porch and mow the lawn.

'Mum, Rupert's dad is only picking me up, not bringing a guided tour through the place,' said Jemma, as the doorbell rung later.

Mrs Farrant eyed Jemma up and down. 'You're getting thin, darling – I must get you a bottle of tonic.'

People were noticing. She was in heaven. 'I'm fine, Mum,' said Jemma. 'Just losing all that puppy fat.'

Mrs Farrant nodded in acceptance, and opened the front door.

Rupert stood on the doorstep, grinning broadly.

'Now isn't this nice?' gushed Jemma's mum. 'I was just saying to Jemma, it's so nice to feel that she is going out with such a suitable sort of lad, although of course she's much too young to have a boyf–'

'MUM!' hissed Jemma. When would she ever learn?

When they reached the Point Eight cinema, Rupert bought a huge bag of caramel popcorn which he insisted on sharing with Jemma. Of course, the diet was very firm about popcorn, but Jemma simply took handfuls and gradually let the kernels fall to the floor. Halfway through the film, Rupert took Jemma's hand. It was cold and clammy but after all, thought Jemma, at least a boy was holding her hand and that had to be a step in the right direction.

As they piled out of the cinema, Rupert said, 'Let's get a coffee while we wait for my father.'

They collected their cappuccinos and sat by the window.

Rupert's eyes seemed fixed on a point midway between Jemma's chin and her waistline. She felt somewhat uncomfortable.

'So where do you go to school, then?' she asked, in an effort to shift his attention.

'Framchester College,' said Rupert. 'I'm a weekly boarder. Four generations of Kentigan-Frys have been educated there, you know. My great-grandfather was the first and he went on to be captain of cricket – and then . . .'

'That's nice,' said Jemma, who hadn't counted on a potted history of his family tree.

'Where do you go – Hendon Hall? Quinton Gate?' Rupert named a couple of what Jemma's father termed rearing grounds for the mindless aristocracy.

'No, Lee Hill,' said Jemma. 'I started there when we moved up from Brighton last summer.'

'Lee Hill?' said Rupert in amazement. 'The grotty comprehensive?'

'It's not grotty,' she said crossly. 'It's great.'

'But a comprehensive? Don't you get some awfully dire types there?'

'Not all comprehensives are peopled with druggies scrawling graffiti on the walls, you know,' she said. 'I've got some really good friends there.'

'All the same, gorgeous girl like you . . .'

Jemma was slightly mollified. No one had called her gorgeous before. And the diet wasn't even over yet.

Rupert stretched his hand across the table and took hers.

'Look, my parents are giving a bit of a do for my sister Sophie – her eighteenth birthday. Course, the proper bash isn't till Christmas when Victoria – that's my other sister – gets back from her year in Switzerland, and there'll be a dance – you know the sort of thing.'

He spoke as if people went hurtling off to balls every few days.

'Anyway, Sophie wanted something on the day, so there's going to be a family supper party at the house in a couple of weeks time. Pa said it might be fun for you to come along as my partner. You could meet my mother as well.'

He looked at her earnestly through his specs.

I've been asked out twice in one week, thought Jemma. I must lose another half stone by then.

Chapter Forty-Four
Jemma Gets Roped In

Jemma couldn't wait to tell someone all the details of her date with Rupert and the upcoming ball. First thing the following morning she was on the phone to Laura.

'But Laura, what shall I wear?' she pleaded, after giving a run down of what he said and what he wore and how he seemed to really fancy her — and leaving out the bit about the clammy hands. 'I really need your advice — I told Mum about the invitation and she actually suggested cutting down one of her old cocktail frocks for me. Can you imagine?'

Laura giggled.

'Yes, but I don't like what I see! Anyway I was about to phone you,' she continued, 'I want to ask you a favour. Are you free this evening?'

'Yes, I guess so,' said Jemma, 'Why?'

Laura told her.

'Do you really think that's wise?' asked Jemma.

'Yes, of course it is — I've checked it out,' said Laura. 'Pleeeease, Jemma — Mum and Melvyn are going to some stupid film about childbirth and I need to do it while they are out. Pleeeeeease. Tell you what — you say yes and this afternoon, before we start, we could cycle over to Boughton and suss out the place.'

'OK,' said Jemma, 'if you're sure. I mean, I don't think it's really necessary. And what if it doesn't work?'

'It will, it has to,' said Laura. 'See you about three o'clock – but not a word to Mum.'

Chapter Forty-Five

Bilu Makes Plans

Bilu only had three days for half-term, and he was spending them with the Banerjis. Truth to tell, he was a bit miffed that none of the guys at school had asked him to their homes. Sumitha's family were very charming and all that, but so provincial and he was bored rigid.

Chitrita was out teaching English to a load of idiot women, Rajiv was at the hospital and Sumitha had gone to sort out her costume for that dumb school play. He was supposed to be keeping an eye on Sandeep till Chitrita got back. Who did they think he was? Some sort of unpaid babysitter? He wanted something exciting to happen, but that was unlikely round here. Even though Mr Banerji agreed to him taking Sumitha out, they had to say it was to a film or the skating rink. If only he could take her somewhere really exciting, show her that there was more to life than Daddy's rules. He needed to get her to unwind and she wouldn't do that surrounded by her friends at some stupid juvenile club. He would just have to make it happen. And Sam Bonner's party next Friday might just be the chance. Now there was a thought. If only he could swing it. He could get out of this boring hole – and get Sumitha just where he wanted her.

He started some careful planning.

Chapter Forty-Six

Talking Man to Man

While Bilu was working out a plan of action, Jon was wondering how to broach the all-important subject with his father. They were at the driving range attached to the golf club and Henry had been going on about grips and swings and keeping shoulders still for what seemed like ages.

'This is thirsty work, Dad – can we go for a drink?' asked Jon.

'Good idea,' said Henry, and they headed for the club house.

While they were waiting for their drinks, Henry spotted a friend.

'Archie, old chap, let me introduce you to my son, Jon.'

Archie was a corpulent man with a fascinating collection of chins and eyebrows like scrubbing brushes.

'Oh, this is the famous Jon – we've heard all about you. You're going to take the art world by storm, I gather,' he boomed.

Jon blushed. 'Well, I don't know about that . . .'

'Oh, yes, very talented, my boy,' said his father, picking up his bitter and Jon's Coke and manoeuvring them on to a table. 'Gets it from the wife, you know – she's shortly to open her own design consultancy.'

'Really?' said Archie.

That's news to me, thought Jon.

'Oh yes. Of course, she'll need a lot of backing from me and I shall handle all the business side for her – she may be artistic, but lousy with figures. But then, women are, aren't they?'

Archie and Henry had a mutual titter over the short-comings of the female sex and then Archie waddled off to regale some other poor unfortunate with his eagle at the 11th.

When they had settled at a table, Jon said, 'Dad, what's all this about you helping Mum? I mean, I know she's had the odd idea about running a business one day, but I didn't think you were that keen on her doing this course, never mind making a career of it.'

Henry took a swig of his beer.

'Well, I can't say I was over the moon at the idea at first, but she has a talent. Of course, I spotted it ages ago, you know, but you can't force these things. No, I've not said much yet, but with someone like me behind her, she

122

could do very well, advising home owners on style, doing up country homes, that sort of thing.'

'But this course, Dad,' said Jon, 'Doesn't it bother you? Her spending time with all these guys from college?' Jon was careful to emphasise the word guys.

'Oh, well, your mum has always been the gregarious type,' said Henry, apparently missing the point. 'Gets on with everyone. I was like that once,' he added wistfully, 'till my life became nothing but work, work and more work. But that's got to change. And your mother's little enterprise could be just the thing to pay for all those little extras.'

Jon sipped his Coke thoughtfully.

'Jon,' said his dad suddenly, 'do you think I look – well, do I look old for my age?'

Jon looked up in surprise.

'I've never thought about it,' said Jon. 'No, I don't think so. You look about fifty and that's what you are.'

Henry sighed. 'But I'm overweight,' he said.

'Yes,' agreed Jon.

'Oh,' said his father who had been hoping for a staunch denial.

'You could always get fit, though,' said Jon. 'Join a gym, get a tailor-made fitness programme.'

It was then he had his flash of inspiration. 'Tell you what, Dad, why don't we both go? We could do it at the weekends and one night a week. Come on.'

This could be just what they needed, him and Jon, thought Henry.

'You don't mind?' said Henry. 'Being seen there with your old dad?'

'No, it'd be cool,' said Jon. And if we get you in trim, Mum might stop lusting after college students so much, he thought to himself.

Chapter Forty-Seven

How the Other Half Live

'It's massive!' gasped Jemma, as she and Laura jumped off their bikes a few yards short of the entrance to Boughton Hall. 'I can't go to a do there – they probably all wear tiaras and have servants and . . .'

'Get real – of course you can go!' said Laura. 'And tell me every detail. It can go in the novel. My heroine, Lady Lavinia, has just fallen in love with Jonquil Descartes – I could have them living somewhere like this after the wedding, and they can discover it's haunted, and then Lady Lavinia can have a horrific accident . . .'

'Laura!' Jemma laughed. 'We are supposed to be sorting my social life, not writing your blockbuster. What *shall* I wear?'

'Oh, it won't be that grand,' said Laura airily, as though she attended formal dinners every day of her life. 'I reckon a silvery satin slip dress with strappy sandals and a choker – yes, that'd be good.' She eyed Jemma up and down. 'You've lost a lot of weight, haven't you?'

Jemma couldn't have been happier if David Beckham had kissed her. Someone else had noticed.

'Come on, let's get back and do my hair,' said Laura, jumping on her bike and pedalling like fury off up the hill.

Jemma followed, panting hard. She was sure this hill was steeper than it used to be. There was a nasty buzzing in her ears and her legs felt like jelly. Luckily, at the top of the hill, Laura stopped for a swig of orange juice from the bottle in her saddlebag.

'Just think what it must be like to live in a place like that,' panted Jemma as she took a swig offered by Laura.

Which was just what Laura was thinking. There was Rupert Kenty-whatever swanning about in that mansion, while she, Laura Turnbull, was stuck in some miserable semi in a godforsaken close in town with a pregnant mother and her moronic lover. Fate could be very cruel.

Chapter Forty-Eight
In Pursuit of Beauty

That evening, after Laura's mum and Melvyn had left for the film, Laura and Jemma grabbed a handful of towels from the airing cupboard and ensconced themselves in the bathroom.

HAIR-WE-GO
Raven Raver
Permanent Hair Colour with Added Gloss
Before use, test on strand of hair.

'Right,' said Laura, peering at the instructions on the bottle of hair colour, 'it says here you have to be sure to cover every bit of your hair with the dye, right down to just above the roots. I'll lean over the bath and you can put the rubber gloves on and massage it in.'

'Are you sure this is wise?' said Jemma, pulling on the gloves. 'It looks awfully black in the picture.' She was secretly wondering how black hair would go with Laura's ginger eyebrows and mass of freckles but decided it was better to say nothing.

'Well, that's the colour I want it to be!' snapped Laura. 'I tried being subtle and it doesn't work – I put those comb-in highlights in and no one even noticed.'

'Oh – I thought your hair had just gone lighter in the sun,' said Jemma.

'No, courtesy of Streak It On. This time, I am going to be totally transformed,' declared Laura, clamping a towel to her face and bending over the bath. 'Get on with it, then,' she said in muffled voice.

'Have you done the strand test?' queried Jemma.

'Oh no, I haven't got time to mess around with all that,' said Laura impatiently. 'Just get on with it and then we can make a coffee while it does its thing.'

By the time they had had a drink, read that week's copy of *Yell!*, discussed the various outfits Jemma could buy for the big party and debated whether Bilu really was two-timing Sumitha, it occurred to Jemma that they had forgotten all about the hair.

'Hey!' she gasped. 'How long has that stuff been on your hair? We forgot to time it – the leaflet says to leave it on for fifteen minutes.' They dashed to the bathroom.

'Rinse thoroughly until the water runs clear,' Laura read. 'Go on, I can't wait to see it.'

Five minutes later, with Jemma chewing her lip anxiously behind her, Laura stood up and turned to gaze at her new radiant self in the mirror.

'Oh no!' she squeaked. 'What's happened?'

All over Laura's head were broad streaks of khaki green hair. The rest was a dull charcoal colour. It looked a total mess.

Tears trickled down Laura's face.

'It's all gone wrong!' she sobbed. 'What shall I do?'

'Don't worry,' said Jemma. 'Let's try using loads of shampoo and see if we can get some of it out. After all, it's supposed to fade each time you wash it.'

Half an hour, six shampoos and five clean towels later, the result was just the same.

'I'll never be able to show my face outside the house again!' wailed Laura. 'What do I look like? Oh, Jemma, what am I going to do?'

Jemma was at a loss.

'Your mum'll sort it out,' she said. 'She's bound to know what to do. And talking of mums, I'd better go. I promised mine I wouldn't be late – Gran's arriving tonight.'

What Jemma didn't say was that she felt really weak and wobbly. And hungry. She had only had one satsuma and three pieces of crispbread that day and thought that maybe she should eat something. She'd have an apple when she got home.

After Jemma had left, Laura sat on the edge of the bath and cried. So much for stunning Jon with her looks. If he had any sense, he would never be seen within a million miles of her ever again. Her life was over. She might as well just curl up and die.

By the time Laura's mum and Melvyn returned home, Laura was in bed with a pillow over her head.

'Laura's asleep early for half-term,' remarked Ruth, switching on the kettle and making herself a chocolate spread and banana sandwich, her latest craving.

'Mm,' agreed Melvyn. 'Are these the house details you

picked up?' he said, pointing to a pile of estate agents' leaflets.

'Yes – take a look at the one in Berrydale,' said Ruth. 'It looks lovely and it's not too badly priced.'

'I think,' said Melvyn, 'we should put this house on the market tomorrow. I'll pop in to Homefinders tomorrow morning and get them to come out and do a valuation.'

'Brilliant,' said Ruth. 'In that case, I had better spend tomorrow morning cleaning. So it's bed for me. Being pregnant seems a lot more tiring than it used to be.'

Melvyn decided to take a shower. Which was tricky because he couldn't find a single clean towel anywhere. When he opened the airing cupboard, he discovered a heap of soggy towels with grey streaks all over them. He surveyed them thoughtfully, sniffing each in turn.

He crept across the landing and opened Laura's bedroom door a chink. She was sound asleep, but it only took one glance to see what had happened. And to take in Laura's tear-stained face and the extraordinary colour of her hair.

'Everything all right?' said Ruth sleepily as Melvyn climbed into bed.

'Fine,' he said. It might be politic to try to sort this one himself.

Chapter Forty-Nine
A Helping Hand

At eight-thirty the following morning, Melvyn knocked on Laura's door.

'Go away.' Laura sounded as though she had a very bad cold.

Melvyn pushed the door open a chink.

'Laura, can I come in for just a minute?' he asked.

'No, you can't.'

'It's concerning the little matter of black towels,' he ventured.

Silence.

'And your hair,' he whispered.

No comment.

'And I'm leaving for work in fifteen minutes and I thought we could go via that Fringe Affairs place and I could drop you off for some repair work,' continued Melvyn. 'My treat, needless to say.'

Laura gulped. Was there a glimmer of hope after all?

She opened the door and Melvyn tried very hard not to laugh. She was wearing black trousers and a black sweater, and her head was swathed in an assortment of coloured scarves like a gypsy setting out for the fortune telling booth.

'I suppose you think this is really hysterical!' said Laura, choking back tears.

'No, I don't,' said Melvyn seriously. 'I think you feel silly and miserable and fed up and worried about what everyone will say. Which is why I thought a trip to the hairdresser's sooner rather than later might be a good idea. I'm sure they deal with things like this all the time.'

'And you'd pay?' queried Laura.

'Of course,' said Melvyn. 'By the way, as yet your mum doesn't know anything about it. I'll whip the towels into the washer while she's in the shower.'

Laura looked at her feet.

'I would have done them but . . .' she began.

'I know, I know – last night was not the best moment of your life, was it?' he said. 'So let's get going?'

'What's in all this for you?' asked Laura suspiciously.

'Oh, Laura, why do you always have to think that people have ulterior motives? Doesn't it ever occur to you that I am doing it because I care about you and because I can guess how you feel right now?'

He handed her a wad of notes.

'There's forty pounds – that should cover it, but if not, tell them I'll call in with the rest in my lunch hour.'

Laura smiled through her tears.

'Thanks ever so much,' she said.

Perhaps, she thought, he wasn't quite such a geek after all.

★ ★ ★

'Morning. Welcome to Fringe Affairs. How may I help you-oo?' The girl on reception chanted the words like a mantra.

'I'd like to talk to someone about my hair,' said Laura. 'It went wrong.'

Two and a half hours later, Laura gazed into the mirror. Her hair was a deep shade of muted copper, cut into a chin length bob.

'It really suits you,' said the hairdresser. 'Very sophisticated. I've cut off all those frizzy ends and sorted the colour, but you'll have to keep conditioning it.'

'I love it,' said Laura. 'Thanks ever so much – you've saved my life!'

'Just don't go messing with dyes on your own – promise!' said the stylist, laughing. 'Oh, and I'm afraid that'll be forty pounds.'

'Oh, it's OK, my . . . my mum's boyfriend is paying,' said Laura.

'Lucky you – that kind of guy I could do with in my life,' said the hairdresser.

As Laura stepped out of the salon, she almost bumped into Melvyn.

'Hi,' she said.

'Do I know you?' asked Melvyn in mock surprise. 'I dropped off some funny kid with streaky hair and frizzy ends; now I collide with this chic sensation!'

Laura laughed. 'Is it OK? Do you like it?'

'It's great,' said Melvyn, chuffed that his opinion should matter. 'You look a million dollars. Want a lift home?' he added.

Laura nodded. 'But shouldn't you be at work?'

'I am allowed a lunch hour, you know,' Melvyn said, smiling. 'Besides,' he added as they walked to the car, 'I've got to pick up some keys from Homefinders.'

Laura looked at him questioningly.

'There's a house in Berrydale that your mum and I are going to see this evening – want to come? I rather think we need more space, what with the three of us, and a new baby, don't you?'

'Oh yes, yes – but why didn't you tell me?' said Laura, climbing into the car. 'I'm always the last to find out things.'

'Actually,' said Melvyn, 'I did try to mention it over a certain Sunday lunch but you bunked off before I . . .'

Laura looked guilty.

'I suppose I've been a bit of a pain to you, haven't I?' she said.

Melvyn smiled. 'Well, let's just say I like it better when we're talking. I rather guess your mum will too. Now, shall we go home?'

Chapter Fifty

An Offer You Can't Refuse

Sumitha and Bilu were watching television.

'Bilu, I saw you the other day with a girl outside the Contrary Cockerel. Who was she?' Sumitha's heart was thumping. She wasn't sure she wanted to know the answer.

Bilu thought fast. 'Girl?' he said in a puzzled voice. 'Oh, her. Natalie. Poor kid, she was in an awful state. Her dog had been put down that morning.'

Sumitha breathed a sigh of relief.

'So – she's not a girlfriend of yours?'

Bilu laughed. 'Girlfriend? Heavens, no, I hardly know her. She's the sister of a mate of mine from school. I just tried to cheer her up. Anyway, why would I want anyone else when I've got a gorgeous girl like you?'

Sumitha glowed.

'So gorgeous that I want her to come to a party with me on Friday. My mate Sam is having a party while his parents are away – should be a really good laugh.'

'It sounds terrific, but I don't know what Dad will . . .'

'Oh, give it a rest,' retorted Bilu. 'All I hear is Dad this and Dad that. You're a big girl now – but if you don't want to . . .'

'I'll come,' Sumitha said quickly. 'But . . .'

'Leave your father to me,' interrupted Bilu, planting a kiss on top of her head.

'So you see, Mr Banerji,' said Bilu over supper that Wednesday night, 'I'd like to take Sumitha with me.'

'Well, I don't know . . .' began Rajiv, looking at his wife. 'She is very young to go to a late function.'

'Oh, I do understand,' said Bilu. 'But you see, some friends of my parents – from Calcutta, you know – are exhibiting in an exhibition of Hindu art and the party is to celebrate the opening. I would so like to introduce Sumitha to them. Do you know the Gangopadhyays?'

'The name rings a bell,' said Rajiv. 'And yes, it is an excellent idea! It is important for you to maintain close links with our culture.'

Got you, thought Bilu.

Hurrah, thought Sumitha.

I don't believe a word of it, thought Chitrita.

Chapter Fifty-One

Thwarted on Every Side

Chelsea was fed up. This was turning out to be a rotten half-term. For one thing, she had phoned Sumitha to invite her over for the day, only to discover she was not in the least bit interested.

'Oh, no thanks, Chelsea,' she said. 'Bilu and I are going to a party and I need to wash my hair and stuff.'

Stuff Bilu, thought Chelsea. That's all Sumitha thinks about these days – no one else seems important to her any more. It was all right for some – whenever she got to go out with Rob, it was with a gang of others and nothing mildly romantic ever happened. Sometimes she wondered just how Rob saw her – she had a nasty feeling she was just one of his many mates. If she could only get him on his own more often, she might be able to win him over.

That's an idea, thought Chelsea, as she hung up. I'll phone Rob. Maybe we can go bowling.

'Oh, I am sorry,' said Rob's mum on the other end of the phone. 'Rob's not in. He's round at Mandy's, practising for the show. Any message?'

Yes, tell him I'm putting a contract out on Mandy blimmin' Fincham's life, thought Chelsea.

'No, it's OK thanks,' she said and put down the phone and burst into tears.

Just then the phone rang. Perhaps, thought Chelsea, it was Rob, just home and desperate to talk to her. It wasn't. It was Jemma who spent the next ten minutes telling Chelsea all about Rupert and his eyes that crinkled at the edges when he smiled and his big house and the forth-coming party.

'So will you come shopping tomorrow and help me

choose something to wear?' said Jemma. 'I've got to get it sorted before Mum decides to make some taffeta creation out of her old cocktail frock. And I do want to look really good for Rupert.'

Oh great, thought Chelsea. There's all you lot with impressive love lives – even Jemma – and there's the boy of my dreams snogging that cow Mandy Fincham.

Chapter Fifty-Two

Encounter With the Enemy

'That was great!' said Henry. 'I hadn't realised that working out could be such fun. Mind you, I feel like I've tackled Everest without oxygen.'

Jon grinned. 'You'll get used to it – that fitness programme they drew up for you builds up really gradually.'

On the drive home, Henry said, 'I was telling old Peter Hall down at the club about you; now his brother is deputy editor of *Shire News* – he might be able to get you some work experience with their design team in the holidays.'

'That would be fantastic, Dad – thanks!' Jon said.

'Well, it would be their privilege. I told Peter you were not just any artistic kid but something pretty hot.'

'Oh, Dad!' Jon exclaimed. Dad might never give up bragging but at least he was on Jon's side now.

Jon's high spirits plummeted when they turned into the driveway of their house.

'Well, now, who's car is that?' mused his father.

The car parked by the garage was strange to Henry, but not to Jon. It was that guy again – the one he kept seeing his mum with.

Before Jon could think of any way to stop him, his father blundered through the back door, hurled his kit on the floor and walked towards the sitting room, where peals of laughter came from behind closed doors. Jon followed close behind.

'Oh, Henry, Jon, you're back!' Mrs Joseph jumped up from where she was sitting on a huge Aztec floor cushion that Jon hadn't seen before. 'Do look what Vernon brought me – he did it in Design. Isn't he a clever clogs!'

Jon's mum had flushed cheeks and shining eyes.

'Oh, I'm sorry – Henry, this is Vernon. We're on the same course. Vernon, my husband, Henry, and this is Jon, our son.'

Vernon jumped up and held out a hand. 'Well, hello there, pleased to meet you both,' he said.

Jon glared at him.

'Can I offer you a drink – oh, I see you've had some,' said Henry, catching sight of an almost empty bottle of Chardonnay on the hearth. 'Well, Vernon, so you're on this course too? Pretty tricky when you've got a regular high-flyer like Anona to compete with, eh? She's quite something, isn't she?'

His wife stood open-mouthed. Henry was actually praising her artistic skills and she hadn't thought he had even noticed she had any. Poor Dad, thought Jon; he worships her and she is treating him like dirt.

'Oh, she certainly is,' said Vernon, nodding enthusiastically. 'Her sense of colour is incredible. Actually, I was just off,' he continued, getting up and brushing invisible flecks off his suede waistcoat. 'Still haven't finished our assignment for Monday.'

If that's not the sign of a guilty conscience, I don't know what is, thought Jon. He's cutting and running because he can't face Dad. How could Mum do it?

'See you again soon,' said Vernon, waving a hand.

Not if I can help it, thought Jon.

Anona gave Vernon a quick kiss.

'And I do hope everything works out for you,' she said.

'Fingers crossed,' said Vernon. 'And thanks for being so great.'

How could she? thought Jon. Kissing another man. And with her own husband in the house. He would never have thought it of her. He felt really sorry for poor old Dad. And very peeved with his mother. She mustn't be allowed to get away with it.

Chapter Fifty-Three

This Desirable Residence

Laura, on the other hand, was far from peeved. She had got home and her mum had been ecstatic about her hair. When she asked how Laura had managed to pay for it, Melvyn simply said, 'I thought she might like a treat – after all, if she's going to be a big sister, she needs to look the part.'

And what's more, Melvyn obviously hadn't said a word about the hair dye, because the towels were blowing merrily on the washing line and her mum was singing along to Radio Two, which would normally have driven Laura mad but which was a welcome sign that she was in a good mood.

Then they had all been to look at the house in Berrydale and Laura had nearly expired from joy. This was more like it. She could fancy living here – it had class. All the houses stood back from the road and they were all different. This one had a gabled roof and a wrought iron balcony over the front door and a big garden at the back. The sitting room was twice the size of their one at home and there were two bathrooms.

'You could throw up in peace!' said Laura to her mother.

'I've stopped all that now,' said Ruth, laughing.

'Well, next time then,' said Laura.

Melvyn and Ruth exchanged glances. Could Laura possibly be accepting things at long last?

'We can have it, can't we?' said Laura. 'Please. And Melvyn does need space for his computer stuff.'

'Well, we've got others to look at,' began Ruth, thinking that Laura had never before cared whether Melvyn was squashed into a shoe box. 'We'll have to see!'

'But this is perfect!' said Laura. 'When my book is published and I become famous, this house would look great in all the press pictures.'

She wondered why Melvyn and her mother both burst out laughing.

Chapter Fifty-Four

Tears Before Bedtime

Sumitha was really excited about the party. Bilu had been very clever – they had gone to the exhibition, which really *did* exist, and which really *was* sponsored by friends of his father. They didn't stay long, simply bought a catalogue as proof to Rajiv of their devotion to Hindu art. Bilu introduced Sumitha to a couple of people. 'Excellent alibis!' he muttered – and then they left for the party.

By the time they got there, Sam's party was already in full swing.

'I'll get you a drink,' shouted Bilu above the noise of the music.

He came back with a bright blue drink in a tumbler and handed it to Sumitha.

'What's in it?' asked Sumitha, tentatively.

'Oh, this and that – go on, it's innocuous enough. Oh hi, Nigel, Chris . . .' and he went across to greet his mates.

Sumitha sipped the drink. It tasted lovely – ice cold and very refreshing. By the time Bilu bought Nigel and Chris over to meet her, the glass was empty.

'Another?' said Bilu with a smirk on his face.

'Great – yes, please,' said Sumitha. She was feeling really good, like she could take on the whole world.

After two more drinks, Sumitha found she could chat about absolutely anything to absolutely anyone. More and more friends of Sam and Bilu kept turning up and she talked to them all. She found everything funny. And they laughed at everything she said. Sam said she was a real gem which made her feel good, and someone else muttered something about lambs to slaughter which made her giggle even more. Then someone fetched her another drink. Bilu took it from her hands.

'I say, I think maybe you've had enough,' said Bilu. Getting her merry was one thing but he didn't want her passing out on him. 'Shall I get you a fruit juice?'

'No way,' said Sumitha, grabbing the glass from him. 'I like these.'

'I'm going to get you a Coke,' said Bilu firmly and pushed his way to the bar.

'What a party pooper!' said a tall guy with piggy eyes next to her. 'I'm Giles – and those cocktails taste even better with sugar on the top – want some?'

Sumitha nodded. He sprinkled some on top for her. It was wonderful. She felt ten feet tall, glamorous and witty. For a while.

'Hi, Sumitha.'

She turned round and tried to focus her eyes. It was Mandy Fincham.

'I didn't expect to see you here,' said Mandy. 'Wouldn't have thought it was your scene at all.'

'Oh, I'm a prate garty poer . . . I mean, a great cratie . . .'

Everyone laughed.

'See who's here, Rob,' said Mandy. 'It's Sumitha.'

Rob? thought Sumitha. I wonder if Chelsea knows he's here. And with Mandy Fincham at that.

What's Sumitha doing at a party like this? thought Rob. Come to think of it, what am I doing at a party like this? Everyone was at least eighteen or older and there seemed to be mountains of alcohol everywhere and proper bartenders mixing drinks.

Bilu reappeared carrying a large glass of Coke.

'Drink this,' he said.

'No,' said Sumitha, 'I wanna dance.'

'I don't think that would be a good idea,' said Bilu.

'Well, I want to dance so there,' said Sumitha whose head felt as though she had been on Space Mountain three times.

'I'll dance, kiddo.' Giles dragged her on to the floor.

Normally Sumitha loved dancing. She was good at it and had an inborn sense of rhythm. But tonight her feet kept doing things they shouldn't and the more Giles spun her round the worse she felt.

'I think I'd like to sit down now,' she gasped, after a few minutes.

Bilu appeared at her elbow. 'Giles, stop it – I reckon she's smashed.'

'I need to sit down,' she said. 'Stop please.'

But the words came out all funny. Everyone laughed and the sound echoed in her ears as if she was in a long tunnel.

'Stop it, for heaven's sake!' she heard Rob shout. 'She's had too much to drink – stop it – leave her alone!'

Her head felt as if it was floating away from her body. And then she was horribly sick.

Sumitha staggered into the bathroom with Bilu following. She felt awful. And right now, she didn't want Bilu. She wanted her mum.

'You were sick all over my shoes,' said Bilu in disgust. 'They cost over two hundred pounds.'

'I feel awful,' she said.

'You'd better get her home, Bilu,' said Nigel who had come to see what was going on.

'You've made a right mess on my parents' carpet,' said Sam. 'It's Chinese and cost a fortune.'

'That'll teach you to consort with kids,' said Giles. 'Anyway, where's Natalie?'

Natalie? thought Sumitha. That was the girl . . . but before she could think anything else she was sick again.

'Oh great,' said Bilu. 'One decent party in a boring half-term and you have to go and spoil everything. You're pathetic, you know that?'

All the way home in the car Sumitha wanted to die. Her head was swimming and funny colours kept flashing before her eyes. Once she thought she saw a big green bird on the bonnet of the car and another time she saw two of everything. It was horrible.

Bilu was driving really fast, grumbling about his ruined evening, and slamming the gears, apparently not at all worried that her stomach felt as if she had spent all afternoon at Alton Towers and her eyes refused to focus. She wished she had never gone to the stupid party.

Bilu wished he'd never bothered with her. In the seat beside him, Sumitha groaned. She did look awfully pale and pinched. He guessed he shouldn't have given her those drinks in the first place, but they weren't that strong, and how was he to know she would go on slurping them indefinitely? And it wasn't as if anyone had given her

145

anything else. Unless . . . Bilu took a deep breath. Now if that had happened, he was going to have to do some pretty quick thinking before confronting Mr Banerji. And they were practically home.

'I'm stopping for petrol,' he said to Sumitha as they pulled in to the service station. 'It's only a few miles, but I don't think I have enough.'

He leaned across and kissed her on the cheek. 'Feeling better?'

'No,' she said. His breath smelled foul. He jumped out of the car and lurched a little unsteadily towards the pumps. Sumitha, who up until now had felt too out of it to think straight, realised he shouldn't be driving.

'I'm going to the loo,' she muttered as Bilu unhooked the pump.

But she didn't. She walked into the service station, took out her mobile and phoned home. She swayed from side to side as she waited for an answer and had to hang on to the wall because everything round her appeared to be moving . . . she just prayed it would be her mother.

'Yes?' said her mum's worried voice.

'Mum? Mum, it's me. Oh Mum,' she sobbed, 'please come and get me.'

Sumitha sat huddled at a corner table in The Country Kitchen café at the service station.

When Bilu had come searching for her, she had told him about her phone call home and he had flipped.

'You stupid kid!' he shouted. 'If you had done what I said, we'd have got away with it. Well, you can stay and take all that's coming to you, but I'm off.'

'Bilu, you can't!' cried Sumitha. 'Don't leave me – and don't drive. Please.'

But Bilu had gone.

Tears ran down Sumitha's cheeks.

When Rajiv and Chitrita hurried into the café, Sumitha leaped up and hurled herself into her mother's arms.

'Oh Mum, I feel so awful – I keep being sick and I wanted you and I can't see properly and . . .'

Chitrita hugged her.

'It's all right, we're here now. We'll sort it all out.'

'Where is Bilu?' asked Rajiv grimly.

'Gone,' said Sumitha.

'What do you mean, gone?' asked Rajiv.

'When I said you were coming, he just shouted at me and left,' said Sumitha tearfully.

'I see,' said Mrs Banerji. 'So as well as being irresponsible, he is also a coward.'

'Mum, I feel . . .' and with that Sumitha fainted at her mother's feet.

147

Chapter Fifty-Five

A Day of Reckoning

24 Wellington Road,
Leehampton
LE3 INS

Dear Bilu,

I am writing to say that sadly you will not be welcome in our home in future. And while you may consider that my decision is a direct result of the foolish and irresponsible way in which you caused Sumitha to become drunk when at the party that is only a part of the story.

To make a mistake is part of growing up. To run away from your mistakes and expect someone else not only to take the blame but to face the music alone, is despicable.

You lied to my wife and myself; you abused our trust. You put Sumitha's life, and your own, at risk by driving when you had been drinking. Sumitha naturally admired you and envied your rather questionable lifestyle. It seems that even she has realised that there is more to life than fast cars and stylish nightclubs, that things like trust and caring for the well-being of others are what make a man.

I can only hope that one day you discover this
for yourself.
Your cousin,
Rajiv Banerji

At ten the following morning there was a tap on Sumitha's door. It was her mother.

'Come downstairs, please. Your father and I want to talk to you.'

Oh no, thought Sumitha. Here it comes.

'I've got a bad headache,' she ventured.

'I don't doubt it,' said her mother.

Sumitha pulled on her dressing gown and padded downstairs. At least this morning the staircase was stationary.

In the dining room, her father was sitting at the table with his head in his hands. Her mother sat down opposite him, and coughed.

He looked up.

'Sumitha,' he said.

Sumitha took a deep breath and waited for the diatribe.

'I am sorry,' said her father.

Sumitha looked puzzled. 'Pardon?' she said.

'I am sorry,' he repeated. 'I have been misguided and although you acted very foolishly last night, and I am very angry about your deception, I feel partly to blame for what happened.'

'But Dad . . .' began Sumitha.

'No,' he said, holding up his hand, 'just listen. This is

not easy for me. For many years, I have believed that everything that comes out of India is good. Superior to England. Bilu was Indian; I assumed he upheld all that was best in our culture.'

He sighed. 'And I suppose, I have been suspicious of many aspects of Western life. Because of that, I have always tried to keep you and Sandeep close to our old traditions. Now I realise that there is good and bad in everything – and that not everything Indian is good.'

'What your father is trying to say, Sumitha,' interjected her mother, 'is that, although what you did yesterday was wrong and misguided, he feels that if he had let you do more of the things your friends do, you might not have been quite so bedazzled by Bilu. He is, after all, a person-able boy and you wanted to be grown up and have a boyfriend like the rest. Am I right?'

Sumitha nodded.

'Now Sumitha,' said her father, 'I want you to answer my next question truthfully. Did you take any drugs last night?'

Sumitha gasped. 'No, no honestly. Bilu just kept getting me these drinks – they were blue and tasted nice, really nice. I truly didn't realise they were alcoholic. It wasn't until I stood up that I felt odd.'

'But Sumitha,' said her father, 'your mother tells me that the doctor who saw you in Casualty last night thinks you must have had some illegal substance in that drink. If you know anything at all you owe it to us to tell us.'

'No, Dad, really –' she paused. 'Except . . .'

'Yes?' encouraged her mother. 'Go on, you will not be punished for telling the truth.'

'Well, now I come to think of it, one of Bilu's friends said that the drink would taste even better with a sprinkling of sugar on the top.'

'Oh Sumitha,' began Chitrita, 'Don't you see? That was probably some awful drug or other.'

Sumitha began to cry. 'I didn't realise, honestly I didn't. I'm not going to die, am I?'

'No,' said her mother. 'They said you only had a small amount and because you were so sick, most of it has cleared out of your system. Let it be a lesson to you.'

'Oh and Sumitha,' said her father. 'Bilu will not be welcome in this house any more. I'm sorry – I know you were fond of him but . . .'

'It's all right, Dad,' said Sumitha. 'At least you care. Which is more than he did. But I did love him so.' And she ran out of the room before they could see her crying.

Chapter Fifty·Six

Food for Thought

CHIC
The Parade
Leehampton

RECEIPT

Silver slip dress – size 10	£29.99
Strap sandals – size 4	£25.99
Silver Hoop earrings	£ 4.99
Total	£50.97

'You looked amazing in that dress,' said Chelsea to Jemma as they walked home from town. 'I cannot believe how much weight you've lost, Jemma. Jemma?'

'I don't feel very . . .' began Jemma and fell in a dead weight at Chelsea's feet.

'It's lovely having you here, Mum,' said Mrs Farrant to Jemma's gran over coffee.

'Mmm, it's great being here and seeing you all again,' murmured Gran. 'But I must say I am worried about Jemma.'

'Jemma? Why? She's doing awfully well at school, and having fun with the musical and . . .'

152

'Oh it's not that – what I'm worried about is the fact that she seems to be . . .'

Just then the bell rang. Mrs Farrant opened the door to find an exceedingly white Jemma being held up by Chelsea.

'Sorry, Mrs Farrant,' gasped Chelsea, 'but I had to get a taxi to bring Jemma home and I haven't enough cash to pay for it.'

'Leave this to me!' bustled Jemma's gran. 'Take Jemma inside, dear, and I'll sort the fare. No better still, you hop back in the taxi and I'll get the driver to take you home. It was so good of you to look after Jemma.'

Mrs Farrant took Jemma's arm.

'Petal, what is it? Have you got a bug? Do you feel sick? Oh, dear, dear – before you go, tell me what happened, Chelsea?'

'Well, we'd finished shopping and were waiting for the bus and Jemma just sort of fainted. I'll ring you later, Jemma, to see if you're all right,' said Chelsea.

'Thanks, I'll be fine now,' said Jemma weakly.

Mrs Farrant bustled into the kitchen and poured Jemma a glass of water.

'Oh, in the name of heaven, Claire,' snapped Jemma's gran, coming back into the kitchen. 'She needs more than water. It's as plain as the nose on your face – the child's been crash-dieting. Haven't you, Jemma?'

Jemma nodded and sipped the glass of water. She still felt really weird.

'What do you mean, dieting?' asked Claire, injured that her mother appeared to be taking over.

'Not eating enough,' said her mother succinctly. 'I noticed it within hours of getting here. Jemma, just what have you eaten today?'

'I had an apple for breakfast,' said Jemma.

'And yesterday at supper?'

'Oh, yesterday we had fish pie, and carrots and peas and then I made this lovely syrup tart and . . .' interrupted Mrs Farrant.

'Jemma – what did *you* eat yesterday?' repeated her gran.

'I had the vegetables,' said Jemma.

'But darling, I served you myself.'

'I gave half to Sam and put the rest in a poly bag when you went to answer the phone,' admitted Jemma. 'But Mum, I've got to get really slim for this party. And besides, boys like thin girls.'

'Rubbish, fiddlesticks and total nonsense,' said her gran. 'Boys like girls with sass and a sense of fun – and you can't be lively on an apple and the odd carrot.'

'Rupert keeps staring at me – I know it's because I'm so fat,' whispered Jemma. And she burst into tears.

'Now listen, Jemma,' said her gran, putting an arm round her shoulders. 'In my experience – and yes, I do have a little, old though I may be now – the usual reason why boys stare at girls is because they are besotted by bosoms. And because their testosterone levels are whizzing through the roof,' she added wryly.

154

'Mother!' gasped Mrs Farrant.

'Well, it's true, Claire. Oh, stop looking so shocked – don't forget, I remember you and Jeremy Bayliss-Smith!'

Jemma perked up.

'What, Mum and a boyfriend?' she asked.

'Yes, when she was fifteen this lad at the church had a crush on her. She used to read the lesson and he almost fell out of his pew in adoration. She had a wonderful bust, as I recall. I was quite envious, seeing as all I was endowed with was two undersized thimbles.'

Jemma giggled. Her gran was so funny.

'Jemma, darling,' continued her gran, 'you and I are going to sit down and draw up a sensible eating plan. You mustn't lose any more weight – promise me that. Or you will be ill. I mean it, I've seen it happen. My friend Beryl's granddaughter ended up in hospital because she starved herself. You don't want that to happen to you, do you?'

Jemma shook her head.

'Now go upstairs and get washed and come down and eat a proper meal. All right?'

Jemma nodded. In a way, she even felt quite relieved.

Chapter Fifty-Seven
Recipe for Success

'It's starting!' called Barry. 'Quickly, everyone, I'm on!'

Mrs Gee and Chelsea put their heads round the door.

'Welcome to this week's round of Superchef. *Now in the Red Kitchen we have Anna Standen from Wittersham, in the Blue Kitchen Joan Holman from Eastbourne and in the Green Kitchen, it's Barry Gee from Leehampton.'*

'What did you have on your head, Dad?' said Chelsea, flopping down in front of the fire.

'We all had to wear those hats – hygiene,' explained her father.

'Now Barry Gee will be cooking a wild mushroom consommé with olive croutons, followed by venison with black pudding and a swede purée . . .'

'Yuk,' said Chelsea.

'. . . served with cabbage in garlic and juniper, and to round it off, what will you be giving us for dessert, Barry?'

'A champagne and apple sorbet with a cassis sauce,' said Barry.

'Sounds super tantalising,' enthused Liam Frosby the presenter. *'So on your marks everyone – let's get cooking.'*

'He looks really professional,' said Mrs Joseph to her husband who was watching over in Billing Hill.

'Poncy thing for a man to do,' grunted Henry, and

retreated behind his *Golf Monthly*. A thought struck him. 'Do they have contests like that for designers?' he asked. 'Now you should go on something like that, show the world your talents – you could end up as artistic adviser to an international . . . what's the matter?'

He couldn't understand it when his wife said, 'Oh Henry, you are funny.' But he rather enjoyed the affectionate kiss on the top of his head.

'I hope he wins,' said Ruth to Melvyn. 'He's such a nice guy.'

'True, but just don't expect me to start doing something creative with celeriac,' he replied, smiling.

'The judges found it so hard to place these three in order of merit,' said Liam Frosby. *'But at the end of the day, the winner by just one point was . . .'*

Throughout Leehampton, people held their breath.

'Gee! Well done, Barry.'

The camera panned in on Barry. In his sitting room at home, his wife and daughter were leaping up and down and hugging him.

'Why didn't you tell us you had won?' said Ginny.

'I told you, we weren't allowed to on pain of disqualification,' said Barry. 'And besides, knowing you, it would have been splashed all over the *Echo*.'

'So now, Dad, you can get a proper job as a head chef in a swish hotel, and ditch that awful lorry.'

'Not so fast,' said her father, laughing. 'That was only round one. There's the semi-final and final to go yet.'

'You'll win, Dad,' said Chelsea. 'You're bound to. I'm really proud of you.'

Well now, thought Barry, there's a turn up for the books. There's a first time for everything.

Chapter Fifty-Eight

How Are the Mighty Fallen!

'So how was the party, Sumitha?' asked Chelsea as they waited for the rehearsal to begin.

'Did you paint the town red?' asked Jemma.

'No, she coated the carpet with sick!' tittered Mandy Fincham, twirling round on the stage. 'Had any good cocktails lately, Sumitha?'

'Oh just shut up, can't you?' Sumitha looked close to tears.

'What would you know about anything?' said Jemma to Mandy.

'Oh didn't you hear? I was there. With Rob,' she added, casting a sneering glance at Chelsea. 'Honestly, it was pathetic. She made a right exhibition of herself. No wonder Bilu's gone back to Natalie. At least she's not a

158

wimp. Not, of course, that he ever gave her up,' she added unkindly.

Sumitha tried hard not to cry.

'Ah, diddums – can't hold her drink and can't face the music afterwards. How sad,' sneered Mandy.

'Oh get lost, Mandy!' shouted Chelsea.

Mandy shrugged, pulled a face at Sumitha and wandered off.

'What happened, Sumitha? Who's Natalie?' said Laura.

'It was awful,' said Sumitha tearfully. And told them the whole story.

'What a jerk!' said Laura when Sumitha told them about Bilu driving off into the night.

'I suppose you all think I got what I deserved,' she said. 'I honestly thought Bilu loved me. I never realised that he was just messing me around. I feel so stupid.'

'It could have happened to anyone,' said Chelsea. And we did have our suspicions and didn't say anything so it's our fault too, she thought.

'You weren't to know that those drinks were that strong,' said Jemma sympathetically.

'I'd never had alcohol before, not even at home – what with my dad not approving,' said Sumitha. 'I didn't even know what it tasted like. I don't think I ever want it again. Do you promise you don't hate me?'

'Of course we don't,' said Laura giving her a hug.

'The only person I hate round here is Mandy flaming Fincham,' muttered Chelsea. 'Not only does she consort with the boy I fancy but she's horrid to my friend. I wish she'd drop dead.'

In fact, Mandy was at her most demonstrative during the rehearsal, singing, clapping, throwing her head back so that her hair fanned out behind her. Rob gazed at her adoringly, till Mr Horage had to remind him that Bill Sykes was supposed to be a violent, sadistic man. Mandy laughed and said, 'Must be my charms putting him off.'

Chelsea could have willingly throttled her.

'Up on the table, Mandy, for the dance sequence,' instructed Mr Horage, reading his stage directions.

Mandy leaped on the table and bellowed out,

'Oom pah pah, oom pah pah, that's how it goes,'

Oh drop dead, thought Chelsea.

'Oom pah pah, oom pah pah, everyone knows,

They all . . . AAAAAAAAAAHHHHHH!'

Her foot shot out in front of her and she fell off the table into a heap on the floor.

Serves you right, thought Chelsea.

'Are you hurt, Amanda?' said Mr Horage, who was prone to use full names when stricken. He beckoned anxiously to Miss McConnell who was doing something artistic with a tankard and a few sunflowers.

It soon transpired that Amanda was not all right. She couldn't move her left leg and she was as white as a ghost. When the ambulance men arrived, they pronounced her leg well and truly broken.

I didn't mean it, God, thought Chelsea in a panic.

'I should never have made her dance on the table top,' moaned Mr Horage.

'She'll miss *Oliver!*' gasped Laura.

I've put a curse on her, thought Chelsea.

'Well, at least we've got Jemma,' said Mr Horage, stoutly. 'She'll rally to the cause, won't you, Jemma?

Miss McConnell pursed her lips and looked worried. Jemma Farrant was a nice enough kid, but so quiet and reserved. Hardly the type to play the raucous Nancy. She raised an eyebrow in the direction of Mr Horage.

'Oh no,' said Jemma. 'I can't, sir, honestly, I can't.'

'You can, Jemma Farrant,' said Mr Horage. 'And what's more, you will.'

'But Gran, I can't do it!' wailed Jemma that night, when she'd told everyone about her new role. 'I only agreed to understudy the part because I was sure I wouldn't be needed.'

Her gran put down the *Giant Atlas of China* and gave her a hug.

'You'll be terrific, Jemma,' she said. 'I just know you will bring the house down.'

'But the part of Nancy is not my sort of part,' insisted Jemma. 'You know, all bouncy and extrovert and confident and stuff. That's not me.'

'Who says?'

'Well, everyone always says I am quiet and sensitive and . . .'

'Jemma, the worst mistake any of us can make is to be

161

simply what we think other people want us to be,' declared her gran. 'If I had done that, I would probably be in some rocking chair knitting balaclavas for sailors. Instead, in three months and two days I shall be sailing up the Yangtze.'

Jemma grinned. 'But you're different – you're mad.'

'Thank you darling, that's the nicest compliment anyone has paid me for a long time,' said her gran. 'Now, do you want to do well as Nancy?'

'Of course I do.'

'Then you will,' said her gran.

Chelsea and Laura were in Laura's bedroom packing her china pig collection into boxes ready for the move.

'I can't wait,' said Laura, wrapping her Giggling Piglet in bubble wrap. 'Just think, a decent sized bedroom, two bathrooms – it'll be bliss!'

'Mmmm,' murmured Chelsea. 'Of course,' she added wickedly, 'if your mum hadn't fallen for Melvyn, you would still be living here.'

Laura grinned at her. 'Yes, well, he's not so bad, really – I'm managing to lick him into shape.'

'Do you think,' said Chelsea, 'that Jemma will be OK as Nancy? I mean, she's lovely and everything, but she's not exactly your forceful type, is she?'

'No,' agreed Laura, 'but she's got a terrific voice. I never knew she could sing like that.'

'Me neither,' agreed Chelsea. 'But I still don't think she'll be raunchy enough for Nancy. Still,' she added to herself, 'I don't have to worry about Rob with Jemma playing opposite him. She's just not his type at all.'

Chapter Fifty-Nine

Party Politics

Jemma was too busy for the next ten days practising the role of Nancy and worrying that she would forget her lines or that her voice would be too soft, to worry too much about dieting or to give a thought to the coming party. So when Rupert phoned her the Thursday before and asked her to arrive between seven and seven-thirty, she flew into a panic.

'My dress – what if it doesn't fit now you are making me eat fattening stuff again?' she said to her mother.

'Jemma, it will fit – and I am not making you eat fattening stuff – just seeing that you follow Gran's list. After all, you can hardly call prawn salads and breast of chicken and pork escalopes fattening, can you?'

'But my hair – what'll I do with my hair?' she said, tugging at her mousy brown tendrils in disgust.

'Well, petal, I could do it in a nice little plait or perhaps bunches,' Mrs Farrant began.

Her gran interrupted. 'No, I know. Why don't you go to the hairdressers on the morning of the party and get them to do it? After all, you want to look grown up for an eighteenth birthday do, don't you?'

Claire took a deep breath. 'Good idea, Mother,' she said.

'Try that place, Fringe Affairs, where Laura went. She looks lovely,' she added, turning to Jemma. 'I'll pay.'

Mrs Farrant dropped Jemma at the door of Boughton Hall.

'Have a lovely evening, darling,' she said. 'And don't forget to say . . .'

'Mum!'

'Sorry, love. I'll pick you up at midnight.'

'You're sure I look all right?' queried Jemma, touching her new crinkle perm.

'You look stunning,' said her mum. And meant it.

Rupert opened the door.

'Hi, there,' he said. 'Gosh, you look really great. Love your hair.' He put an arm round her shoulder and led her through to the drawing room. Jemma's heart was thumping so loudly that she was sure everyone assembled in the room could hear.

'Ma, this is Jemma Farrant,' he said. An enormous bust arrived, shortly followed by the rest of Mrs Kentigan-Fry, who was built like a galleon in full sail.

'Lovely to meet you,' murmured Mrs Kentigan-Fry. 'Oh Selena, my dearest, and dear Benjamin . . .' and she bowled off across the room.

'I thought you said it was just a family supper party,' gulped Jemma, gazing round the room at the groups of elegantly dressed guests.

'Oh, this is nothing,' said Rupert airily. 'Oh look, there's my sister with her boyfriend, Felix. Come and meet them.'

From then on, he tugged Jemma hither and thither introducing her every time as 'my girlfriend, Jemma'. She was thinking that it was quite nice to be someone's girlfriend when she heard a whisper behind her.

'She appears to have forgotten to put her dress on.' Giggles followed. 'Why has she come in her petticoat?'

'Oh don't be horrid, Felix, it's one of those slip dresses – Essex girls love them! Ha! Ha!' The laugh that followed sounded like a horse with laryngitis.

'Isn't she the comprehensive kid Rupert was going on about? She's frightfully Top Shop, isn't she?'

'Ya, well my brother is so damned wet, he wouldn't manage to hook any kind of classy girl.'

Jemma wanted to die. She'd felt so good in her new dress till then. How was she to know that everyone else would be dressed up to the nines in designer frocks?

Supper was even worse. There were so many different knives and forks. Jemma just watched Rupert and prayed she did the right thing. She felt people's eyes on her everytime a new course was served. The guy on her left kept saying things like, 'Were you at Klosters last Christmas?' and laughing like a drain when she said 'Where's that?' and the girl opposite, who was called Lucinda Pinkerton-

Danesby or something weird said, 'Not Klosters for her, Clacton more like.'

She was beginning to wish she hadn't come when Rupert's father, who was sitting at the top of the table said, 'So what do you do in your spare time, Jemma?'

'Oh, er, well at the moment I am busy rehearsing – our school is putting on *Oliver!* and I've got to be Nancy because the girl who was doing it broke her leg.'

'Splendid, splendid,' said Sir William. 'Well, good for you. Putting your free time to good use.' He shot a critical glance at his daughter who was giggling with Felix. 'Always enjoyed am dram myself, you know.'

'Gosh, that's terrific – I'll come and watch you,' said Rupert.

His mother looked at him as though he had suggested personally supervising the digging of a sewer.

'Oh wow, how exciting!' said his sister, giving a mock yawn behind her immaculately manicured hand.

After supper, Rupert led her through the house to the conservatory.

'We can dance here,' he said. 'Away from everyone else.'

And he clasped her to him, almost suffocating her, and began to bounce unrhythmically from side to side. He was hot and sweaty but at least they were out of sight of all his sister's pompous friends.

'I'm sorry if I let you down,' muttered Jemma apologetically. 'I mean, not wearing the right sort of dress and things.'

'Oh, golly no. I like your dress – especially this bit,' and he clamped a clammy hand on her left boob.

'Stop it!' said Jemma, whose nerves were already on edge. 'How dare you?' She slapped him round the face.

Rupert went scarlet and stared at her. 'I say,' he began.

'No, *I say*,' shouted Jemma, real anger suddenly taking hold of her. 'Just because I'm not one of your public school friends and don't go around in designer label dresses and own half of Leicestershire, doesn't mean I don't have feelings! I felt really awful in there. And you didn't do anything to stand up for me. I've only just realized what you were up to – you brought me here so your friends could make fun of me.'

Rupert bit his lip. 'I say – I'm sorry. Don't go,' he said as Jemma turned to go back into the house.

'I've never had a girlfriend before, you see,' he admitted. 'I mean, all the chaps at school, they talk about their bits of . . . their girlfriends, and I have to pretend I know all about it. I thought girls liked – well, you know, that sort of thing.'

Jemma felt quite sorry for him.

'Well, we don't,' she said. 'And you might have stopped your sister from being so bitchy to me.'

'Sorry!' said Rupert again. 'She's always so rotten to me I suppose I never notice her any more.' He looked crestfallen. 'I suppose you won't let me kiss you now,' he said mournfully. 'I had hoped you could be my first kiss.'

'Well,' said Jemma. She rather thought it was time she got kissed – she had heard enough over the past few months of Bilu's lips and Chelsea's commentary on the number of seconds her mouth was clamped to Rob's.

'All right,' she said.

'Oh gosh, yes, well,' stammered Rupert, and pulled her to him.

Jemma closed her eyes and waited.

Well, she thought, as a wet smack landed somewhere between her chin and her nostrils. If that's kissing, I honestly don't know what everyone is on about.

'Good evening, was it, darling?' asked Gran the next morning.

'It was OK,' said Jemma.

Her gran regarded her quizzically. 'But?'

'Nothing,' said Jemma.

Chapter Sixty

A Star Is Born

GOOD LUCK!
To my darling Jemma,
The most wonderful girl
in the world.
I'll be rooting for you!
Loads of love
Rupert.

Despite feeling sick with fear and shaking like a leaf, Jemma grinned. The card was attached to the biggest bunch of roses she had ever seen. No one had sent her flowers before, let alone roses. She just wished she felt more – well, romantic about him.

Then she remembered that in a little under fifteen minutes she would be on stage as Nancy and all thoughts of love and passion went out of her mind.

'I can't do it. I can't. I am going to be sick,' wailed Jemma. She was breathing in while Miss McConnell laced her into her scarlet and black dress.

'Of course you can, Jemma,' she said, sounding considerably more confident than she felt. 'You've got a great voice.' *At least that bit's true*, she thought. *She just needs to loosen up a bit.*

'Just *be* Nancy, think yourself into the part and forget

169

everything else. And remember, don't be so gentle in the fight scene with Bill Sykes. He's compromising you, making you his plaything – fight back. Live it,' Miss McConnell suggested.

'Yes,' said Jemma meekly.

It won't work, thought Miss McConnell. Why did Mandy have to break her leg?

'You look great in this dress,' Miss McConnell said truthfully. 'You need a good bust for a dress like this.'

Maybe I'm not so hideous after all, thought Jemma and held her head a bit higher.

Just then, Laura and Chelsea came bursting into the dressing room bearing a huge envelope.

'This is for you,' they said.

It was another card with a picture of a teddy bear and the words 'You can do it!' on the front.

'Thanks a lot – but I can't. I know I can't,' wailed Jemma.

Sumitha was on stage, singing *Consider Yourself* with James Gill who was playing Oliver. Her heart wasn't really in it. She'd imagined that come the big night, Bilu would be out front watching her and she'd be able to sing some of the songs straight to him. It had been a very romantic image. Now she had no one. What's more, Mandy Fincham had told practically the entire school about the disaster at the party and wherever she went, people said things like, 'Fancy a drink, Sumitha?' or 'Heard of any good hangover cures?' She felt she couldn't look anyone in the eye. Everything had gone horribly wrong. No one would want her now. Ever.

Jon was in the third row, watching Sumitha's every move. She was gorgeous. He sighed. There had to be a way of getting to see her again. Bilu or no Bilu.

'*I'd do anything for you, dear, anything,*' sang Jemma, her voice wavering slightly on account of the ten thousand butterflies lurching from her stomach to her throat. I think I am going to die, she thought.

She's going to blow it, thought Miss McConnell.

Don't let me down, Jemma, prayed Mr Horage silently. I know you've got it in you – somewhere.

'*For you mean everything to me,*' she sang a bit more.

It was getting easier.

That's better, thought Miss McConnell.

She's doing it, thought Laura.

Then the dance routine began. It was really quite fun.

And another verse.

And she'd done it. The first song was over.

The applause was enormous.

'She's incredible,' said Mr Farrant.

'I never knew she could sing like that,' said Mrs Farrant, dabbing away a tear.

'There's a lot about our Jemma that you didn't know,' said her gran.

'She's lovely,' said Rupert, his eyes fixed on Jemma's cleavage.

In the wings, Chelsea and Laura were jumping up and down in excitement.

'She's great,' said Laura.

'And her best solo is still to come,' said Chelsea.

In the interval, as Chelsea was changing into her flower seller's costume, Laura came bursting into the library, which was doubling as the girls' changing room.

'Guess what!' she cried. 'Your dad's out there!'

'Well, so I should hope,' said Chelsea. 'I had to suffer watching him marinating mushrooms in front of the entire universe, so he can do his bit.'

'No, I don't mean that!' said Laura. 'He's dressed up as a street seller. He's ringing this bell and selling soup!'

'Oh my sainted aunt!' Chelsea ran through to the stage and peeped through the curtains. There was her father, hat askew, ladling out soup into paper cups with a queue stretching to the back of the hall.

'Chelsea Gee!' shouted Mr Horage, who was feeling a little frazzled what with the pressures of the evening. 'You know the rules: no opening of curtains during the interval. Now get ready for the *Fine Life* number.'

But Chelsea had seen enough. Never mind 'It's a fine life!' As far as she was concerned, hers was a total mess.

Jemma was even better in the second half and was really beginning to enjoy herself. *'If you don't mind having to do without things, it's a fine life!'* she bellowed, picking up her skirts and twirling her ankles. She danced over to Rob, sitting moodily as Bill Sykes at the trestle table and tickled him under the chin. She winked flirtatiously with the boys in the chorus. This acting was great — you could be anyone you wanted to be, she thought.

When they got to the bit in the show where Nancy had to fight with Bill Sykes just before he killed her, she remembered Miss McConnell's advice and she recalled the instance with Rupert in the conservatory. Poor Rob nearly forgot his lines as Jemma dealt him a sharp slap on the cheekbone.

She got a standing applause at the end.

'You were wonderful, darling!' Jemma's gran gave her a bear-like hug. 'I knew you could do it!'

'Well done!' said her dad, 'I didn't know we had a star in our midst!'

'It was fantastic!' said her mother. 'Now petal, I think you should take that stage make-up off right away — you know how sensitive your skin can be.'

'Oh Mum!' chided Jemma, 'it's my face and I'll sort it later.'

'Did you enjoy it, Rupert?' asked Jemma.

Rupert nodded enthusiastically.

'Are you staying for the party? said Jemma, somewhat unenthusiastically. The more she saw of him, the more wet he seemed, and she wasn't too sure she wanted her friends to meet him.

'Oh rather,' he said.

'Dad, what in the name of heaven were you doing, selling soup here?' Chelsea rounded on her father two minutes after the last curtain call.

'Great idea, wasn't it?' said her dad. 'It's raised sixty-five pounds for the PTA as well as making some cash for me and guess what? Mr Todd has given me permission to park in the quadrangle every lunchtime on my way back from the industrial estate. You lot can start eating proper food for once instead of wasting all your money on crisps and chocolate bars!'

'You,' spluttered Chelsea, 'are going to be here? Every day? Selling soup?'

'Yes,' said her dad.

'My life,' said Chelsea, 'might as well be over.'

Sumitha was changing into her jeans. She wasn't going to the party; she had asked her mum to take her straight home. She knew that if she stayed someone would make snide remarks about her, and what's more, everyone else would have a partner. Mandy Fincham was there, all plastered up on crutches and playing for sympathy, ready no doubt to take the mickey. She picked up her bag and headed for the door.

★ ★ ★

'Oh, it's Jon Joseph, isn't it?' Mr Horage beamed at him. 'You're joining us next year, I believe.'

'Yes sir,' said Jon.

'Jon helped me a lot with the designs for the posters and stuff,' said Laura.

'Great stuff,' enthused Mr Horage. 'Quite a little team, the pair of you made,' and he bustled off to chat up Miss McConnell whom he secretly fancied.

'Thanks ever so much for helping,' said Laura.

'That's OK, I enjoyed it,' said Jon. 'Took my mind off my mother.'

'Pardon?' said Laura.

Jon hadn't meant to let that slip out but suddenly he found he couldn't change the subject.

'She's having an affair,' he said miserably. 'With a guy from the college.'

'Are you sure?' Laura gasped. Mrs Joseph didn't seem the flighty sort. Unlike her mother.

Jon nodded. 'I keep seeing them together, and she invites him round to the house, and stuff. She doesn't even try to hide the fact,' he added.

'Then she probably isn't,' said Laura sensibly. 'I mean, she's not going to carry on under the same roof as your dad, is she? Even my mother waited till my dad had moved out before taking up with Melvyn.'

Jon looked hopeful. 'You reckon?'

'Well, why don't you ask her? If she is, it might shock her into stopping. Sometimes parents need us to keep them in line – they hit this middle-aged bit and go all weird. It takes someone with their feet on the ground like us to help them back on course.'

Jon looked much more cheerful.

'I will, I'll do it tonight,' he said. 'You're really easy to talk to, you know that?'

Laura inwardly preened.

'Oh, and by the way,' he added, 'when do you think Sumitha will turn up?'

Rob was standing in a corner chatting to Jemma and Rupert. Chelsea dashed up and flung her arms round his neck.

'You were brilliant,' she said; planting a kiss on his cheek. 'And you, Jemma.'

'Thanks,' said Jemma. 'This is Rupert, by the way.'

Chelsea looked at him as he held out a cold clammy hand. He wasn't exactly an oil painting but he probably had a sparkling personality.

'Gosh, hello,' said Rupert.

Apparently not, thought Chelsea. What does Jemma see in him?

At that moment, Mandy Fincham hobbled up on her crutches. 'Hi,' she said breezily. 'Rob, you were brilliant. Especially since you had to make do with an understudy playing opposite you.'

'Jemma was great,' said Rob defensively.

'Oh yeah, for a beginner she muddled through OK,'

conceded Mandy. And she looped her arm through his and laid her head on his shoulder.

'Oh, get lost, Mandy,' said Rob, and shrugged her away. 'Go and find someone else to throw yourself at. Come and get some food, Jemma – you deserve it.'

And while Mandy, Chelsea and Rupert stared open mouthed, he led Jemma to the buffet table.

'Hey, er, hang on a moment, old chap,' blustered Rupert. 'That's my girl. You can't just . . .'

Jemma turned to Rupert.

'No, I am not your girl,' she said pleasantly. 'Or anyone else's for that matter. I'm me and even if I choose to eat a sausage roll with a little green man from Mars, that's my business, not yours.'

Rob discreetly backed off and went to join Jon, Chelsea, and Laura who were straining their ears to catch the rest of the conversation. They couldn't believe that meek old Jemma was saying all this.

'But I thought, I mean, I want you for my girlfriend,' said Rupert.

'Oh, and what you want, you always get, do you?' said Jemma. 'Anyway, you don't want me. You just want to say you've got a girl.'

And come to think of it, she thought, that's why I wanted you. Just to say I had a boyfriend.

'Oh, but I do, I do, honestly,' said Rupert earnestly. 'Even when Mummy said that you weren't our class and that I could do much better, I told her you were ace.'

'Oh, she did, did she?' said Jemma. 'Well, you can tell Mummy from me that no girl with half a brain will want you until you stop treating all females like walking mammary glands. In short, until you grow up. Good night,' and with that she walked away.

Rupert stood staring after her.

'Oh bother,' he muttered.

'You certainly sorted Mandy out,' said Chelsea, who was a little worried by the way Rob kept looking at Jemma.

'She just irritated me in the end,' he said. 'She took too much for granted.'

Ya boo shucks to you Mandy Fincham, thought Chelsea triumphantly.

'I'm glad we're back together again,' she murmured.

Rob looked at her and took a deep breath.

'Look, Chelsea, you're great, you're a laugh and I like you loads,' he said. 'But – well, I mean, I don't see us as an item. You're a great mate, I mean that, but no more than that. I'm sorry, I should have said before, but – well, to be honest, you're not my type – you're just too much of an extrovert for me, I suppose. Like Mandy, you just come on too strong. Sorry.'

And he strolled off to join Jemma.

Chelsea choked back tears. How could he? She hadn't come on strong. Had she? Yes, she had. It was all her mother's fault. Chelsea had started to act like her and what had it got her? Rejection, social annihilation and shame. She re-thought her plan for the evening: go home, curl up and die.

Chapter Sixty-One
Jon Gets It All Wrong

When Jon got home, Vernon was just leaving.

'Well, how are you, Jon?' he said pleasantly. 'Had a good evening?'

'Yes, not that it has anything to do with you,' snapped Jon.

'Jon!' said his mother.

Jon pushed past them and went into the kitchen.

Two minutes later, after waving goodbye to Vernon, Jon's mother appeared.

'I cannot believe what you just said to Vernon,' she expostulated. 'How could you be so rude to . . .'

'To your lover?' shouted Jon. 'Is that what you want to know? How could I be so rude to your lover? Well, quite easily as it happens!'

'I *beg* your pardon?' Anona's eyes widened.

'Oh, don't beg *my* pardon,' thundered Jon. 'It's Dad you should be apologising to. Every time he's out, you have that – that lascivious jerk round here. How could you, Mum? How could you do it?'

'Do what?' said Anona.

'Carry on with him when you are married to Dad? Don't you care about him? About me?' Jon had a horrible feeling he was going to cry.

Anona burst out laughing.

'Oh great, you think it's funny, do you – wrecking lives?' Jon shouted.

His mother sighed. 'Jon, will you listen to me?' she pleaded. 'It's not like that.'

'Oh no?' said Jon, unable to stop the flow of his bottled-up feelings. 'Well, that's how it seems to me. I've seen you with him. Oh yes, all flirty and giggly going into the Antique Gallery, walking round town like two starstruck kids. What do you see in him? How could you fancy him?'

'For the last time, I don't fancy him!' shouted Anona.

'Oh, pull the other one! And anyway, he fancies you!' shouted Jon. 'It's obvious.'

Anona smiled. 'No, Jon,' she said. 'Vernon does not fancy me. Not remotely. He doesn't fancy me or any other woman for that matter. He's gay.'

Jon gaped. 'What?'

'Vernon is gay. He has been going through a rough patch lately. His partner left him a couple of months ago and he was really upset. He sank himself into the course, and we got to working together on a couple of projects.'

Jon felt mildly foolish. And very relieved.

'Really?'

'Really,' said his mother. 'He comes round here some-times when your father is out because it stops him brooding. And it helps. He is much better at everything than I am.'

'And you still love Dad? He's trying to get fit so you will fancy him again.'

Anona looked amazed. 'He said that?'

'Well, not exactly,' admitted Jon. 'But I know he is. And I'm glad you're not having an affair.'

Anona smiled at him. 'Perhaps we should all be sure of our facts in future before we jump to conclusions?'

Jon looked abashed. 'Sorry,' he said. 'But it did seem . . .'

'Appearances,' said his mother, 'can be deceptive. Remember that.'

Chapter Sixty·Two

All Girls Together

'Is Rupert still pestering you?' Chelsea asked Jemma. It was the Sunday before Christmas and they were all over at Laura's new house, helping her get her room straight.

'He sent me this card telling me his life was desolate

without me,' said Jemma, grinning and stacking books in Laura's new pine bookcase. 'I felt like sending one back with the word *TOUGH* in capital letters on the front!'

Jemma felt it best not to add that she had also received a card from Rob inviting her to a New Year's Eve party. She didn't know what to do. Chelsea had been mad about him and she didn't want to fall out with her. She couldn't *believe* that anyone could fancy her rather than Chelsea. Not that she was bothered about having a boyfriend any more. She was more excited about the drama lessons her gran was giving her for Christmas.

'I don't miss Bilu like I thought I would,' said Sumitha, handing Laura a large pink china pig. 'But I do miss having someone special. I should have realised Jon was worth fifty of Bilu when I had the chance. Sorry, Laura, no offence meant.'

Laura shrugged. 'Well, you can have him,' she said valiantly. 'There's no point my holding out hopes there. He spent the whole party after *Oliver!* asking where you were.'

'He did?' said Sumitha, brightening visibly.

'Yes,' said Laura shortly. It was one thing being magnanimous, and quite another having it rubbed in.

'I wish I hadn't blown it with Rob,' said Chelsea, sighing. 'There'll never be anyone else like him, ever. I shall probably spend the rest of my life alone.'

'You'll meet someone else soon,' said Jemma. 'Besides, boys aren't all they're cracked up to be.'

'That's right,' said Laura. 'Boys are just not worth the bother. From now on, I shall devote myself to writing,' she added loftily.

'You're right,' said Chelsea. 'Who's that?' she added, pointing out of the window to where the most gorgeous guy, with blond, wavy hair and an incredible bum was carting a Christmas tree up the driveway.

'I don't know,' said Laura. 'But since it would appear he lives next door, I intend to find out. Fast.'

She headed for the door. Chelsea followed close on her heels.

'I thought,' Jemma called after them, 'you weren't interested in boys any more.'

'That,' said Laura, 'was then. This is now. Anyway, Mum wanted me to integrate with the neighbours.'

'Warwick's back – he's brought a friend for Christmas,' said Chelsea's mum when Chelsea ventured into the kitchen that evening.

'Not a girlfriend?' said Chelsea in amazement.

'No, a lad,' said Ginny, stuffing mincemeat into pastry cases. 'Guy Griffiths. He lives in America.'

Oh no, thought Chelsea. Any friend of my brother's will only be interested in potting compost and root grafting.

'And you must be Chelsea?' said a deep gravelly voice. Chelsea turned. And stared in open mouthed wonder.

'Well, hi – I'm Guy,' said the vision. 'I'm afraid I've

descended on you for the festive season. I hope you don't mind.'

Mind? thought Chelsea. You're the best thing Father Christmas has brought in years.

'It's so cool getting to see a real English Christmas,' he said. 'I guess it'll be real different from California.'

That accent, thought Chelsea, is divine.

'Where are all the cool places around town?' asked Guy, perching on the kitchen stool. 'I want to drag that brother of yours away from his begonia seedlings on New Year's Eve and show him a good time. Will you come along and help us out – and bring some girls with you?'

I think, thought Chelsea, I shall leave giving up men till next year.

'I'll have to think about it,' said Chelsea.

She had learned that it didn't do to come on too strong.

'I've thought about it,' said Chelsea, a millisecond later. 'I'll come.'

The Leehampton Series

Also available by Rosie Rushton
from Piccadilly Press:

Meet the girls: Holly, Tansy, Jade and Cleo.
Each book follows one week in their lives –
but what a week! Disasters, parents, secrets,
boyfriends and more challenge the girls.

Four friends. Seven days. About a hundred
things that can (and will) go wrong!

What a Week Omnibus Books 1–3
(What a Week to Fall In Love
What a Week to Make It Big
What a Week to Break Free)

What a Week Omnibus Books 4–6
(What a Week to Make a Stand
What a Week to Play It Cool
What a Week to Make a Move)

What a Week to Take a Chance
What a Week to Get Real
What a Week to Risk It All

www.piccadillypress.co.uk

☆ The latest news on forthcoming books

☆ Chapter previews

☆ Author biographies

☆ Fun quizzes

☆ Reader reviews

☆ Competitions and fab prizes

☆ Book features and cool downloads

☆ And much, much more . . .

Log on and check it out!

Piccadilly Press